S0-BNT-013

"We don't have time for this!"

Tessa's voice rose. "I told you, there are men in masks—"

"I want to believe you," Anthony said. "I really do. Just tell me you'll cooperate."

His free hand moved so quickly she didn't even realize what he had done until she felt the cold sting of metal against her wrists. She looked down. Anthony had handcuffed her.

"Tessa Watson," he said, "I'm arresting you on the charge of obstructing and impeding an official police investigation—"

Emotion overwhelmed reason. She wrenched away from him, turned and ran blindly down the beach, with her hands cuffed.

"Come on, Tessa!" Anthony shouted. "Stop! We found Cassidy's body! She's dead."

She faltered a footstep and nearly fell, as if she'd taken a literal bullet to the back. She turned and saw the sorrow flooding his eyes, as if now that he'd started to tell her the truth, he knew he couldn't stop.

"Tess," he said. "I could get in real trouble for telling you this, but they think you killed her."

Maggie K. Black is an award-winning journalist and romantic suspense author with an insatiable love of traveling the world. She has lived in the American South, Europe and the Middle East. She now makes her home in Canada with her history-teacher husband, their two beautiful girls and a small but mighty dog. Maggie enjoys connecting with her readers at maggiekblack.com.

Books by Maggie K. Black

Love Inspired Suspense

Undercover Protection
Surviving the Wilderness
Her Forgotten Life
Cold Case Chase

Rocky Mountain K-9 Unit

Explosive Revenge

Protected Identities

Christmas Witness Protection
Runaway Witness
Christmas Witness Conspiracy

True North Heroes

Undercover Holiday Fiancée
The Littlest Target
Rescuing His Secret Child
Cold Case Secrets

Visit the Author Profile page at LoveInspired.com for more titles.

COLD CASE CHASE

MAGGIE K. BLACK

LOVE INSPIRED SUSPENSE
INSPIRATIONAL ROMANCE

If you purchased this book without a cover you should be aware that this book is stolen property. It was reported as "unsold and destroyed" to the publisher, and neither the author nor the publisher has received any payment for this "stripped book."

LOVE INSPIRED® SUSPENSE
INSPIRATIONAL ROMANCE

ISBN-13: 978-1-335-58842-5

Cold Case Chase

Recycling programs for this product may not exist in your area.

Copyright © 2023 by Mags Storey

All rights reserved. No part of this book may be used or reproduced in any manner whatsoever without written permission except in the case of brief quotations embodied in critical articles and reviews.

This is a work of fiction. Names, characters, places and incidents are either the product of the author's imagination or are used fictitiously. Any resemblance to actual persons, living or dead, businesses, companies, events or locales is entirely coincidental.

For questions and comments about the quality of this book, please contact us at CustomerService@Harlequin.com.

Love Inspired
22 Adelaide St. West, 41st Floor
Toronto, Ontario M5H 4E3, Canada
www.LoveInspired.com

Printed in U.S.A.

Are not two sparrows sold for a farthing? and one of them shall not fall on the ground without your Father.

—Matthew 10:29

For all those who've made mistakes
and are trying to do better.

ONE

As Tessa Watson stepped off the bus in the tiny town of Princess, British Columbia, her eyes locked on the tall, broad-shouldered man in the cowboy hat who lounged on a wooden bench on the other side of the street. He was following her. She was certain of it. He wasn't the first suspicious character Tessa had believed was spying on her since she'd become a licensed private investigator. She'd opened her own one-woman investigations agency at the age of twenty, almost ten years ago. She'd named it The Chase Agency, in memory of her friend Cassidy Chase, who'd disappeared as a teenager and never been found. In the past few years, Tessa had noticed enough shadowy figures walking behind her down darkened alleys, or hanging around by her parked car, to suspect she'd made at least one powerful enemy along the way who was now keeping tabs on her. Not to mention the occasional threatening letters she got in the mail from unknown sources who wanted her dead.

But this guy—whoever he was—was definitely the most relentless stalker she'd ever had.

Tessa glanced past him, through the lenses of the thick-rimmed glasses she wore to disguise her features, and pretended to scan the quaint stores of Princess's Main Street. Her fingers fiddled with the strings on her sweatshirt, activating the tiny camera hidden in the pocket, and she took several pictures of him, which she would run through facial recognition as soon as she could. Beside the camera, in her breast pocket, sat the most important piece of evidence she'd ever collected, and the clue that had led her to Princess—the engraved silver bracelet Cassidy had been wearing on the day she disappeared. Tessa had spent years searching for it, and she'd suddenly gotten a hit on an online auction aggregate site early this morning. A bangle matching the description had turned up at a pawnshop in Whistler, BC.

The pawnshop owner had warned her she wasn't the only one interested in it, but had promised to hold it for the two hours it would take her to get there. She'd hit the road immediately, feeling fresh hope building in her chest, and then had somehow picked up an unwanted shadow along the way. Was he after Cassidy's bracelet too? Or was he after her? She'd first suspected the cowboy was on her tail when she'd noticed the same blue truck kept reappearing behind her on the highway from Vancouver to Whistler. Then she'd noticed the man himself following her around the mountain resort town. In an all too casual way, he seemed to track her every move without ever getting too close or letting her see his face. She'd managed to ditch him in a parking garage, leave her car there, change her appearance in a washroom and then hop on the bus to Princess instead of driving, in the hopes that would shake him.

Apparently, it hadn't. Instead, he'd beaten her there. He'd even gone to the trouble of swapping the shirt he'd been wearing for a blue plaid one and brown leather jacket, and switched up his baseball hat for a Calgary white hat, as if he was on his way to the Stampede. Despite the palpable shiver of fear that seeing him again spread down her spine, she also felt her lips quirk. This guy was almost as good as her.

Who are you, cowboy? Who are you working for?

Some past criminal she'd taken down who held a grudge? Or had she somehow stumbled into a police investigation so significant they'd actually sent one of the big guns to trail her?

Catching a bus hadn't been part of the plan when she'd left her house this morning. Then again, neither had been trekking all the way to Princess. When Tessa had initially rushed out the door to hop in her car that morning to head to Whistler, a pair of uniformed officers had approached her, pulled out their badges and asked if she was free to come into the local station for questioning. They wouldn't tell her why or what it was about, and she knew the law well enough to know that they didn't have to. But she also knew that she was under no obligation to go anywhere with them unless they detained or arrested her. So she'd gotten into her car, taken off and been relieved that they'd finally stopped following her when she hit the highway. They'd been simple to shake.

Something told her losing this cowboy wouldn't be so easy.

She stretched the handle of her small rolling suitcase out to its full length, raised her chin and walked down the street toward the

Princess Inn. The late morning sun still shone bright overhead. But storm clouds were beginning to build at the edge of the horizon where they brushed against the Rocky Mountains. Gigantic pine trees towered high around the town. There was something about them that made Tessa think of sentry guards, as if the trees themselves were trying to keep someone or something from escaping. The man at the pawnshop had told Tessa the bracelet was discovered by someone camping on a small island nearby. He wouldn't give her the person's name, but claimed this guy had camped at that particular site so often he knew with absolute certainty it had only been dropped there in the past twenty-four hours. Tessa wasn't sure she believed that. But a heavy storm was on its way, and if there were any other clues to Cassidy's disappearance on the island, she didn't want to risk them being washed away by the rain before she could search the area. Thankfully she'd managed to not only book a hotel suite online, she'd even managed to find herself a kayak.

She'd check in, make her way to the island and see what she could find.

Just as soon as she lost the guy on her tail.

She reached the Princess Inn. Chimes jangled as she pushed the door open. For just a fraction of a second she could see the face of the man who'd been following her reflected in the glass. She froze as recognition dawned.

Anthony? Anthony Jones?

Anthony was the one following her?

When they'd been teenagers, Anthony had promised to love her forever. Instead, he'd broken her heart. In an instant, the face disappeared again. Suddenly her heart overruled her brain, and she turned around to look for the face of the man she'd once thought herself so deeply in love with. Instead, all she saw was the man's back as he walked away from her down the street. No. The man who'd been following her couldn't be Anthony. It had been a lifetime since she'd put the earnest young man in her rearview mirror. He'd been eighteen then, passionate about reading books on law enforcement and playing basketball, and unwavering in his belief that he knew what was best in every situation.

No good would come from thinking about him now.

The smell of well-polished wood and vanilla filled her senses as she walked through the lobby. Caribou and elk heads looked down at her from above the check-in desk. They were flanked by mounted salmon. A pair of stuffed and mounted mallards sat on top of a fancy cabinet that held rows upon rows of old-fashioned room keys. A sign on the wall read Hunters Welcome.

She tapped her finger on the bell that sat on the counter, and a satisfying ding filled the lobby. A second later, a man in a waistcoat and with a head of white hair appeared from a door behind the counter.

"Checking in, miss?" He stretched out the syllable of the last word for a beat, as if waiting for her to fill in the rest.

"Galloway," she said. "Joanna Galloway. One night."

She laid a pretty good fake ID that matched her alias down on the table, but the man barely even glanced at it. The suite had already been paid for with a prepaid credit card that couldn't be traced back to her but ensured the inn wouldn't be out a dime. The man handed her a very modern key card, gave her the Wi-Fi password and wished her a pleasant stay. Tessa thanked him, grabbed her suitcase and walked toward the stairs. Her eyes scanned the large picture window and searched the street outside.

The man who she kept telling herself couldn't be Anthony Jones was nowhere to be seen. She'd have felt safer if she'd spotted him there, glaring at the front door and waiting to nab her when she exited. At least then she'd know where he was.

She found her suite halfway down a hallway on the second floor. It was fairly simple. The living area had a couch, table and two chairs. To her right was a bathroom and to the left, the one bedroom with a second adjoining bathroom. Straight ahead lay huge sliding glass doors leading out to a balcony, and beyond that a thick forest of cedar trees. She put her suitcase on the bed, then went into the washroom where she stared at the unfamiliar face in the mirror. First, she took off the long, straight wig she'd been wearing to reveal her usual mass of unruly, shoulder-length brown curls underneath. Then she ditched the glasses she didn't actually need to see. Finally, she swapped her blue sweatshirt for a red one. She shook her hair out, went back into the bedroom, unzipped the suitcase and pulled out the one thing inside—a camo-green backpack that contained all her belongings.

Now what?

Tessa worked her cases alone. But she gathered a lot of help and information from a group of likeminded citizen detectives she connected with online, as well as material she gleaned from community message boards and neighborhood watch groups. She also had a private social media page for past, present and prospective clients. When she'd posted something there, while still on the bus, about needing to rent a boat in Princess, one user had responded immediately, saying she worked for a local mom-and-pop boat rental business and would leave a kayak for Tessa in a nearby cove that was only a few minutes' walk from the hotel.

It had been twelve years since a seventeen-year-old Cassidy had walked out of a Whistler bar with a stranger and never been seen since. She'd been hanging out and drinking, under-age, with teenage colleagues there before she'd gone missing. A couple of brief texts had been sent from Cassidy's cell phone to her parents in the days after her disappearance, reassuring them that she was okay. Then her debit card had been used and her cell phone had pinged around British Columbia and Alberta for weeks after she vanished, and the media had written Cassidy off as a troubled runaway who had a history of underage drinking.

In the years since, Tessa had built a huge database of facts about the case, including in-

terviews and newspaper articles. It seemed the
police had dropped the ball and let the case go
cold, but that hadn't stopped Tessa from calling and emailing law enforcement repeatedly
whenever she uncovered anything new.

What Tessa wanted to do now before heading to the island was fire up her laptop, log on
to the dark web, and take a couple of hours to
review both the maps she'd downloaded of the
area and her files on Cassidy's disappearance,
in the hopes she'd find some scrap of a clue
that would help in her search. She had a tablet with her too, which gave her the opportunity to scan two screens at once and compare
them. That had been her plan before she'd been
facing the twin threats of an impending storm
and an unwanted shadow.

Now she didn't want to risk hanging around
the hotel too long.

She downloaded the photos she'd taken on
the street with her hidden camera. The man's
face appeared on the screen.

A strong jaw. A tender mouth. Eyes hidden
under the brim of a cowboy hat...

Once again her heart told her it was Anthony, and her mind told her heart that it was
wrong. She was only thinking of him because
her mind was stuck in the past, and once she

figured out what happened to Cassidy she'd be able to move on.

Something rustled in the trees outside and drew her attention to the window. A shiver ran down her spine. There was no one there. A reverse image search for the man's partial face turned up nothing. She quickly sent the pictures to her small and trusted group of citizen detective friends, hoping one of them would have more success. Then she pulled out the bracelet and examined it closely. The harsh chemicals the pawnshop had cleaned it with would have probably destroyed any fingerprints or DNA. But she searched for both just in case with a small crime scene kit in her bag and found neither. The bracelet itself was in remarkably good shape, sterling silver with intricate flowers and vines on the outside and an engraving on the inside: To Cass—Friends Forever—Tess.

Ironically, it hadn't felt like it the night Cassidy disappeared. Their friendship had ended in a spectacular fight after Cassidy had decided to get back together with her no-good boyfriend, Kevin Scotch-Simmonds, just days after she'd begged Tessa to sneak out at night to come rescue her from him at a party. Kevin was the son of the owner of Canada's second-largest grocery store chain, and the party had been at his family's spacious summer house. When Tessa had arrived, Kevin had been violent and drunk, and Tessa had been injured in the scuffle. Anthony had come to her rescue, but he'd also called her parents and the police from the hospital. Tessa had been grounded for sneaking out and forced to give up her summer job as a camp counselor.

Tessa and Anthony hadn't seen eye to eye about anything that'd happened that night. Anthony had called Tessa both reckless and foolish. Tessa said Anthony shouldn't have taken charge of everything and called her folks and the cops without talking to her first. They'd broken up. And it had all been for nothing. Cassidy had gone right back to Kevin, told Tessa they could no longer be friends and blocked her number. Tessa had then written Cassidy an angry letter saying all sorts of nasty things she'd regretted the instant she'd sent it.

Then, less than two months later, Cassidy had taken a weekend off work to party at a cottage with five other camp counselors. They'd all gone underage drinking in Whistler and Cassidy had disappeared.

And yet video footage of the bar had shown

Cassidy had been wearing Tessa's bracelet that night. Did that mean Cassidy had forgiven her?

Tessa took pictures of the bracelet from all angles and uploaded them to her online storage drive. Then she locked the bracelet, laptop, her computer tablet and various bits of her disguise in the hotel room safe. It wasn't the best option, considering whoever was following her might break in, but taking them with her seemed even more risky. She cast a final glance around the room to make sure she hadn't left anything behind.

Unexpectedly, a Bible on the nightstand caught her eye. Her ultra-strict parents had raised her to believe in a God who, like them, "loved" her in theory but didn't seem to like her very much. When Tessa had taken a DNA test, she'd been upset to discover her dad wasn't her biological father. Rather than talking with her about it—let alone comforting or reassuring her—her parents been angry with her for even asking them if it was true. They hadn't spoken to her since. But Anthony had believed in a God who really cared about people and wanted them to take care of each other. There'd been something she'd really liked about the way Anthony prayed.

God, if You're listening, help me solve what

happened to Cassidy. I don't need anything for me. Just help me find her. And if something bad happened, help me get justice for her, okay? I'm sorry I wasn't a better friend to her.

She wasn't sure if that counted as a prayer, but it was the best she had for now. Tessa pushed the window open and looked out into the trees. The balcony was only one story off the ground, but it was still farther than she wanted to drop. She'd never been much of a fan of heights. She pulled a climbing rope from the side of her rucksack, clamped one edge on the balcony and made her way down. Hopefully nobody on the first floor was looking out, wondering why a woman was rappelling down the building. She landed in a crouching position and pushed the release button on her rope. It slithered down toward her.

"Tessa!" A familiar voice filled the air. "Tessa Watson! I'm with the RCMP Major Crimes Unit. Just stop right there and put your hands where I can see them. I promise, I only want to talk."

She turned.

It was her former boyfriend Anthony.

He was about twelve feet away from her. The cowboy hat was gone, and as she stared straight into his face, she knew with absolute certainty that, no matter how hard she'd tried to deny her own eyes, she couldn't even pretend to think that it wasn't him. He'd been eighteen when she'd seen him last. Now he was thirty. And not just older, but stronger too. And a lot more rugged, with a touch of premature gray in his dark hair, and a new depth in his clear blue eyes that made her suspect he'd spent the intervening years not just building muscle on the outside but also strengthening who he was at his core.

Slowly, he pulled his weapon and aimed it at her.

"I need you to come with me," he said. "Right now. Police need to question you about a very important open investigation, and I'm not taking no for an answer."

It was said within the RCMP that the reason Sergeant Anthony Jones, of the Unsolved Homicide Unit within Major Crimes, had never lost either a suspect or a case was because he had the ability to calmly talk a leopard out of its spots. Personally, Anthony believed it had more to do with the fact he was a stickler for following the rules. He'd never once pulled his weapon without mentally running a checklist of why it was justified. And now, as he stared into the heart-shaped face of the woman he'd once thought he was going to marry, he started ticking off the reasons why he had to ignore the unexpected flutter in his chest.

Tessa Watson was a person of interest in a homicide case. She'd been traveling in disguise and using fake IDs. She'd refused to cooperate with police earlier and had instead left town. Plus, in his experience, calmly pulling a weapon was normally all it took to jolt someone into realizing he actually meant business. But, as he slowly strode toward her along the side of the building, he watched as her hazel eyes narrowed, and he was suddenly reminded that Tessa wasn't most people.

"I'm not going with you," she said.

He stopped about ten paces away from her. Their eyes locked. She'd changed in the past twelve years. Her long wave of brown curls was now cropped above her shoulders, and there were fresh lines on her face. Back when he'd been a teenager, he'd thought Tessa had been the prettiest girl he'd ever seen. Now she was downright beautiful. He risked another step forward.

"Are you really a cop?" she asked. "I thought you were either going to be a basketball player or going to go into hostage negotiation like your childhood hero, General Alberto Mc-Clean."

She was stalling for time. But that was okay. Suspects did it all the time, and he knew how to use it to his advantage. Still, something about her words made him rock back on his heels. She'd remembered all that? When Anthony was in grade nine, General McClean had been testifying before a Parliament hearing on live television, when a disturbed individual had pulled a gun and threatened to open fire. McClean had talked him into surrendering without incident.

"Turns out it's called the Crisis Negotiation Team, and it's a voluntary unit within the RCMP that only gets called out in case of emergency," he said. "I also coach a basketball team for at-risk youth and play in a pick-up league."

"How's your vertical jump?" she asked.

"Excellent," he said. "But I'm honestly surprised you didn't know I was a cop."

"Sorry, I haven't followed you online," she said. "It was just too hard seeing your face after we broke up, so I blocked you." His instincts told him she was telling the truth. "Did you actually follow me from Vancouver to Whistler, and then here? You could've just picked up the phone and called me."

This from the woman with fake IDs and disguises.

"If I had called, would you have picked up?" he asked.

She pressed her lips together and didn't answer.

"I tried your folks," he added, "but they said you haven't spoken in years." Her folks had always been incredibly strict, bordering on controlling, but they'd loved Tessa and she them. "I'm guessing there's a story there?"

"Not one I'm about to tell you."

Heat prickled at the back of his neck. *Come on, man, keep it professional. She's not the woman you loved. She's a person of interest who your boss thinks committed a murder, and you've put your career on the line to bring her in.*

"There's an important case I'm trying to solve," he went on, "and I think you might have some information that will shed light on it. So, we're requesting you come in for questioning. Immediately."

"The closest RCMP detachment is two hours away," she pointed out. "That's a pretty long drive for a chat." She had him there. "What is all this about, anyway?"

"Sorry, I'm not authorized—"

"I didn't ask what you're authorized to tell me," she interrupted, and her voice rose. "I'm asking you to tell me what's actually going on. I do know something about how this works. I'm investigating—" Her voice hitched, like she was about to say something more and stopped herself. "I'm not going to just head to a police station without knowing why. Especially when I know full well I can then be held up to twenty-four hours without charges. Even if the cop they sent after me is a guy I used to know back in high school."

Used to know? Back then he'd thought they'd been in love.

"Tessa." He heard his own voice sharpen. "This isn't a game. You're a person of interest in a Major Crimes case."

Her eyes widened. "What kind of Major Crimes case?"

He didn't answer. He wasn't authorized to. Thunder rumbled softly from somewhere on the horizon, and he watched as her body tensed.

"And what if I refuse?" Tessa asked.

"I really suggest you don't," he said, "because I won't hesitate to arrest you."

And with that she took off running, dashing through the trees before he even realized what was happening.

"Tessa!" he shouted after her. "I'm not joking! The RCMP will issue a warrant for your arrest!"

She didn't look back. He holstered his weapon and took off after her. Frustration burned at the back of his throat. What was she thinking? His legs were almost twice as long as hers. Sure, she'd taken off at an impressive speed, ducking behind trees and jumping over logs. But it was only a matter of time before he caught up with her again, and then he'd have no choice but to handcuff her.

The Tessa he'd known had always been stubborn and independent. He used to like the fact she looked at things from a completely different way than he did. But the truth was, he'd never been a fan of private investigators. They got in the way of police investigations, skirted the edges of the law and gave victims' families false hope. He knew Tessa meant well. But he'd just told her that she was wanted for questioning in an actual police investigation, and she was acting like it was optional.

Glimpses of the dazzling and dark blue water of the Salish Sea's Georgia Strait appeared ahead through the trees. Just south of Alaska, this stretch of the coast of British Columbia was a maze of inlets and islands leading out to the Pacific Ocean beyond. His footsteps quickened. The trees parted, and he saw Tessa standing on the rocks ahead of him. Then suddenly she was gone. Moments later he reached the spot where he'd lost her and looked down. There lay a tiny cove, no more than a dozen feet wide if that. And there was Tessa, climbing into a kayak and pushing off from shore.

Where had the boat even come from? Did this mean she had an accomplice? His jaw clenched. Even if he scrambled down the rock face and into the cove, there was no way he'd ever be able to catch up with her without getting his hands on a boat somehow. He'd have even run straight for the edge of the cliff and leaped off if he'd had any hope at all of landing in the water anywhere near her. Instead, he planted his feet on the rock, cupped his hands to his mouth and shouted, "Tessa! Don't do this! I promise I am on your side! I only want to help you!"

Was it his imagination or did she flinch?

The paddle seemed to pause in her hand for a fraction of a second, as if she was debating whether to turn back. And somehow he knew that she'd heard him. Then she kept paddling, pulling away from him one strong stroke at a time.

He pulled his cell phone from his pocket and saw that he'd missed a phone call from his boss, chief superintendent of the Major Crimes Unit, Wade Zablocie. Instead of calling him back right away, Anthony snapped a few pictures of Tessa and the departing kayak. He could vaguely make out some kind of logo on the back, which hopefully could be used to identify where it had come from. Then he called his sister.

"Corporal Violet Jones, RCMP Missing Persons." His twin's voice was crisp and professional in his ear.

Six minutes younger than her older brother, with arresting indigo eyes and the same dark hair, Violet was intimidatingly beautiful and also incredibly good at her job. Growing up they'd hung in completely different circles and now worked in different RCMP divisions. He'd always suspected the fact they hadn't always been in each other's faces was part of what had kept them close friends. He also guessed the way she'd answered the phone meant she wasn't alone, considering she'd have seen his name on her call display.

"Hey, Vi," he said, "is this a bad time?"

"Not at all," she said. "Perfect actually. Just give me one moment." He heard the sound of her office chair squeak, followed by what sounded like her placing her hand over the phone and her muffled voice telling someone she'd catch up later. Then her voice was back at full volume. "Hey, Ant, sorry about that. Just had some people standing around my desk I needed to get rid of."

"Are you in the middle of something important?"

"I wish," she said. "Turns out that, thanks to a spectacular mix-up in human resources, the whole division got a prescheduled email blast this morning inviting them to a bridal shower lunch party today, followed by another email not five minutes later calling it off and reminding everyone that I'm not, in fact, getting married this weekend." Anthony winced. It had been three months since his sister's fiancé had suddenly called off the wedding without explanation. "So I've had a steady stream of people dropping by my desk all day checking in that I'm all right."

"I'm sorry," he said. "I know this weekend is going to be a doozy, but I'll do my best to help you through it."

They had a bunch of relatives coming in this weekend, due to nonrefundable airline tickets, and would all be having an awkward party on Saturday thanks to a caterer and reception hall she hadn't been able to cancel either.

"What I need most is a distraction," she said with a strangled laugh. "Tell me you're calling about a case, because I've got nothing active on my desk right now, and I could desperately use something else to focus on."

He sent the pictures to her and almost instantly heard the sound of them ping on her end.

"What am I looking at?" she asked.

"I'm in a town called Princess," he said. "I was just tracking a suspect on foot when she leaped into a kayak and took off. I need to know who rented that kayak and when. My suspect had it stashed in a small cove about a mile north of town."

"On it," she said. He heard the sound of her fingers moving across the keyboard. "Hang on. Is that Tessa Watson?"

He took a deep breath. "Yes."

He glanced back over the water. He could

still see Tessa, growing smaller and smaller as she disappeared toward the horizon.

What are you thinking, Tessa? Where are you going?

"I'm briefing you as a colleague, and for now this doesn't leave your desk," he started.

"Got it."

"Earlier this morning, the Major Crimes' Unsolved Homicide team had gotten a call from a construction crew at a remote cottage half an hour outside Whistler," he said. "A woman's body had been found buried on the property. No ID on the vic yet. But it was the cottage where Tessa's friend Cassidy Chase had been staying with colleagues when she disappeared."

Vi sucked in a sharp breath.

"Which could mean Cassidy was there all along, and we've wasted twelve years chasing cell phone pings, debit card transactions and false sightings across two provinces," she said.

"Yeah," he said. "Major Crimes has managed to keep a tight lid on the news so far. We don't want to tip off whoever did this that we've found her body. But it's only been a few hours…"

"And most lids only manage to stay closed

for so long before things start leaking?" she added.

"Exactly," he said. "Zablocie will hold a full briefing and press conference on it this afternoon."

"Any suspects?" Vi asked.

"The body had a letter from Tessa on her," he said.

"Wow."

"Tessa's been labeled a person of interest," he said. "They want her to come in for questioning. They sent two uniformed cops to bring her in this morning, but she ran. So, I stuck my neck out and begged Zablocie to let me be the one to bring her in. Convinced him that she'd listen to me and I could pull off the impossible."

"As your sister, I have a lot of opinions on this," Violet said, "but they can wait until this is all over. It sounds like you're under the gun."

"He gave me until four."

"And it's about twelve o'clock now," Vi said.

"Yup," he said. Zablocie had given him seven hours, and Tessa had wasted three of them so far with her ridiculous game of cat and mouse. "I'm on pretty thin ice with the chief superintendent over this one. I think he already regrets letting me go after her."

He could hear the sound of his sister typing.

"Next time you talk to Zablocie, ask him how Rapunzel's doing," she said. "It's this goldfish his granddaughter gave him last weekend for his birthday."

He vaguely remembered seeing the elegant black and orange fish swimming in circles in a bowl behind his desk, but he'd never thought to ask its name.

"I think I've tracked down the boat rental place," she added. "Hang on. I'm just going to put you on hold."

The phone clicked and soothing instrumental music crackled down the line.

He closed his eyes and prayed.

God, I could sure use Your help, guidance and wisdom right now. I don't understand what Tess is doing or thinking. But I believe that You understand her even when I don't.

It had been over a dozen years since he'd last prayed those words, but now they came back to him and felt just as familiar, as if he still prayed them every day.

Help me get through to her. Help her to listen, and help me to find the right words to say. Above all, please help me solve this murder case.

"All right, I've got something." His sister's

voice was back in his ear. He opened his eyes. "You still in the woods, on the coast just north of Princess?"

"I am." Still staring out at the empty space on the water where Tessa used to be.

"Okay, I need you to jog north," she said. "You should hit a dirt road soon. Be on the lookout for a large white pickup with a big yellow sunrise on the back. I'll brief as you go."

"Got it." He started jogging.

"So, the kayak was rented by a walk-in customer a few miles north of you, about twenty minutes ago," she started. "He paid cash, and the teenager behind the counter didn't get a name."

"Tessa has an accomplice?" Anthony asked.

Odd. For some reason he'd assumed she'd been working alone.

"Apparently," his sister said. "We don't have a license plate, but she noticed the truck and the direction he headed. Considering the amount of time it would've taken to drive to the end of the dirt road and carry the kayak through the woods, he might still be in the area."

A dirt road appeared ahead through the trees. He ran down it.

"Do we have a description of the guy?" he asked.

"Of sorts," she said. "Apparently, he was tall and very attractive, with a charming smile."

"Hair color? Eye color?" he asked.

"Nope and nope," Violet said. "He wore sunglasses and a hat. There was a tattoo on his wrist that she said was like a bad smudge left over from one he'd tried to remove. And he had a gaiter scarf around his neck."

"I have no idea what that is."

"Imagine the neck part of a turtleneck without the sweater part on the bottom," Violet said. "A gaiter is a circular scarf you can pull up over your mouth and nose like a mask. Some have mouths, animal jaws or other patterns on them. She said his might've been a skull. They're trendy with skiers."

"So, I'm looking for a man who's both handsome and trendy," he said.

He meant it as a joke, but somehow the words sounded bitter as they crossed his tongue. He kept running and started passing remote cottages, spaced out with large swaths of trees between them, and a few vehicles, none of which matched the description. He was about to call it a loss and head back to Princess when he spotted it.

A white double cab truck was parked by the side of the road, a few feet from the edge of the cliff. The beautiful blue stripes and yellow rising sun of British Columbia's provincial flag spread in a decal across the back window, and the license plate was obscured by one of those films meant to thwart speed cameras. It was large enough to haul some serious cargo but had a shine that implied it was a rich man's toy. A guy in a white baseball cap stood by the passenger door with his back to Anthony, and his face was turned in the direction where Tessa had gone. He seemed to be searching the water with an expensive pair of binoculars, and Anthony thought he could see a circular scarf around his neck.

Was this man watching Tessa? Was he her accomplice? Or something else?

He slowed his jog to a professional stride.

"I think I've got him," he told Vi in a low voice. "Expensive truck. Man in a baseball hat with binoculars."

He pulled out his badge and held it aloft.

"Sergeant Anthony Jones, RCMP," he called. "I'd like to ask you a few questions about Tessa Watson."

The man dropped the binoculars, yanked his gaiter scarf up over his face and spun. Anthony caught a flash of the man's face, obscured by mirrored sunglasses and a white mask, patterned like a jaw of menacing teeth.

"I just want to talk," Anthony said.

Too late he saw the gun in the man's hand. He aimed it directly at Anthony's core and fired.

TWO

The bullet struck Anthony just above the heart and embedded itself in his bulletproof vest, spinning him around and knocking him back. Violet was shouting down the phone. His feet slipped out from under him. He stumbled, then fell off the edge of the cliff and down toward the water. His body hit the water and sunk down a few feet into the soft mud below. He struggled to the surface and gasped for breath as he heard the truck peel away above him. Instinctively his hand clutched his chest for the bullet lodged there. It had struck just two inches within the protective cover of his bulletproof vest. If the gunman had aimed just slightly to his left, Anthony would've lost the use of his arm. And if he'd aimed a few inches higher, Anthony would be dead.

He stumbled to his feet and found himself in water up to his waist. He scrambled around for his phone and found it floating a few feet nearby thanks to its waterproof case. The call with his sister was still connected.

He snapped the phone to his ear.

"We have an officer down," Violet was saying. "We need paramedics dispatched on Rural Route Eight north of Princess, British Columbia—"

"Vi!" he said. "I'm okay. Call off the cavalry. I'm fine."

"Are you sure?"

"Yes." Once people were mobilized and on the move it would be hard to recall them. He was fine. The suspect had fled, and he was still intent on going after Tessa himself. For now anyway.

He heard her muffle a sob, but then her voice was all professionalism as she canceled the paramedics. Finally, she whispered a prayer of thanksgiving under her breath. Then she was back.

"Are you okay?" she asked. "What happened? I heard a gunshot."

"He got me right in the vest," Anthony said. "Knocked me backward off the edge of the rocks and into the water. He drove off. Right now, I'm just standing in water up to my waist, trudging back to the closest cove so I can climb back on land. I got the wind knocked out of me, and it's going to leave a nasty bruise. But don't worry. It's fine."

"It's not fine," she said.

No, of course it wasn't. But he'd been through worse than getting knocked back a few feet. It was a setback, nothing more. His phone began to ring with a second call coming through. It was his boss, Chief Superintendent Zablocie.

"Are you sure you don't need additional backup?" Violet pressed.

"No," he said. "I agreed with Zablocie I'm going after her alone. But please put in alert for the suspect and truck, with what limited information we have. Zablocie's calling. I have to take it. Then I have to find a boat and go after Tessa." Not to mention, first he had to get out of this water and make his way to shore. "Are you able to pull up some satellite footage of the area and come up with some idea of where she's headed?"

"I can give you a rough idea," Violet said. "There are a lot of small islands in that area, and I can help you narrow it down."

Hopefully that would be enough. His boss kept ringing.

"I'll also arrange a boat," she added, "and

text you with the details on where you can pick it up."

"Okay, thanks. I'll call you later." He reached to disconnect the phone, but his sister's voice made him stop.

"I know better than anyone how much you cared about Tessa," his sister said, "but whatever she's caught up in isn't worth losing your life over. Promise me you won't do anything stupid."

"I promise."

Then he ended the call and clicked over to his boss.

"Hello, sir," Anthony said.

"Tell me you have Tessa Watson in custody," Zablocie said.

He blinked. So the news that Violet had put out a call for paramedics hadn't made its way back to his boss yet.

"Not yet," Anthony said. "But I'm close."

"We've positively identified the remains found as Cassidy Chase," Zablocie said.

Anthony exhaled as if he'd been sucker punched, even though he'd suspected as much. Tessa would be devastated. Anthony hit a small and muddy cove, climbed onto shore and sat down on a large rock.

"There's an officer with the Emergency Re-

sponse Team named Constable Wilson Newman who has a cottage near Princess," his boss
went on. "I can call him in to help you bring
Tessa Watson in."

"Thank you, but that won't be necessary,"
Anthony said. "To be incredibly honest, I think
if I tell Tessa that Cassidy's body has been
found, she'll be more cooperative. She's been
pestering law enforcement for years to take
another look at this case. She's gathered evidence and sent us clues. If she knew that we
were investigating Cassidy's murder—"

"You're not authorized to tell Tessa Watson anything about this case," his boss interrupted. "Especially the fact Cassidy Chase's
body has been found. You know as well as I
do that the fact somebody is trying to actively
insert themselves in a police investigation is
hardly a sign of their innocence. Sometimes
it means the exact opposite. I have to admit,
I'm disappointed in you, Anthony. You've been
with the unit for almost a decade. Don't come
at me with that kind of rookie stuff."

"But I feel like if I told her something—"

"Anything you tell her could jeopardize the
investigation, taint the interview process and
pollute the evidence we gather." Zablocie cut
him off. He sounded downright irritated that

Anthony was even asking the question. "You know this. When we press charges, we tell them then what they've been arrested for. During the interview process, we strategically disclose whatever information we think will help us get a confession. We have no obligation to tell them anything we don't want to, beyond reading them their rights and offering them a lawyer."

Okay, now he really was talking down to Anthony like he was a rookie.

"I know, sir," Anthony said. "But my gut tells me there's no way she could've ever hurt Cassidy—"

"Tessa Watson is being bumped up from being a person of interest to a suspect," Zablocie said. "The CSIs have managed to patch together more of the letter that was found in the victim's pocket. In it she calls the victim all sorts of unspeakable names. It practically drips with venom."

Anthony pinched the bridge of his nose. Yeah, Tessa had sent him a few letters like that when they'd broken up. When she was angry she didn't hold back and then regretted it later. "But those are just words."

"Sent to a dead woman," Zablocie said. "Look, you've always been an excellent cop, and to be honest I've never doubted your instincts before today. Nobody has your record when it comes to getting confessions and turning criminals. I said I'd give you until four o'clock, and I'll stick to that. You bring her in and come to me with compelling evidence of why Tessa isn't a suspect, and I'll listen. I might even hold off issuing an arrest warrant if she agrees to full cooperation. Otherwise, I'm holding a televised press conference at four o'clock and telling the nation that Cassidy Chase is dead and Tessa Watson is wanted for murder."

Tessa reached the remote island where the bracelet had been found and pulled the kayak up onto shore. The smell of impending rain filled the air. Dark clouds moved across the sun. The storm was on its way much faster than forecasted, and once it hit, it would be relentless. Then all hope of finding any other evidence left behind by whoever had dropped the bracelet would be gone.

And yet, she could feel the guilt of having run away from Anthony weighing her down like there were rocks sitting heavily in her gut. His blue eyes and strong jaw filled her mind. Should she have trusted him? Or even let him take her in for questioning? No matter what differences they'd had, Anthony had always been a good guy who'd wanted the best for everyone. The fact he was now a cop didn't surprise her. What did was the fact he'd trailed her for hours, undercover, and been so good at it she might not have noticed him if she hadn't already been on edge.

The island was much rougher and wilder than she'd expected. From the aerial pictures she'd downloaded she knew the small island had a network of caves underneath the surface, but she hadn't been prepared for just how harsh the terrain would be. Jagged rocks rose high around her, punctuated by thorny brush and twisted trees. She started to climb up the steep ground toward the island's peak, half walking and half climbing. Sharp rocks and nettles dug into her hands. Doubts began to seep into her mind.

Had this really been where Cassidy's bracelet had been found? It was hard to imagine why anyone would ever choose to go camping here when there were so many more beautiful and hospitable islands around. Finally, she reached a flat section of ground where slabs of natural rock spread out beneath her feet with patches of dirt and moss in between, reminding her of a puzzle. A circle of burned wood and charcoal to her right showed that someone had once set a fire there, but she could tell at a glance that it had been days, maybe even weeks ago.

She cast her gaze down around the island in all directions. It was small, but not tiny. It definitely would've been large enough for a few dozen cottages to have been scattered around the coast, each with their own small beach and boathouse, without any one of them ever seeing their neighbors. But only if there'd actually been a single patch of ground that was level enough to build on. There was no way she'd be able to walk the island from one corner to the other, scanning the ground and bushes with a metal detector, or get a usable picture of anything like footprints. She was going to have to regroup and come up with a new plan. But first she'd construct a shelter against the storm.

The island's network of caves had been formed from a now dry underground river that once ran through the earth. They might flood if the rain got heavy enough. So, she pulled a dark blue tarp from her backpack, spread it across the ground and hammered it into the gaps of dirt between the rocks with long metal stakes that were as thin as pencils. Then she got out a dark green pop-up tent, set it up over the tarp and lashed it to two nearby trees. She left the rest of her camping equipment in her bag, except for a tiny flat and circular flashlight, about two inches wide, which she clipped to the inside of the tent flap to fill the space around her with a soft and gentle glow.

Drizzle began to fall. She was sitting just inside the shelter of her tent, looking out at the pale gray sky and planning her next move, when she heard the men coming. A warning shiver ran up her spine. She snatched the flashlight from the tent, switched it off and stuffed it her back pocket. There were two of them at least, maybe more, judging by the number of voices she could hear talking and sets of footsteps she could hear crashing through the woods. Quickly she threw her backpack over her shoulder and then slid a spare tent peg up her sleeve. She dashed out of the tent and ran for the edge of the plateau, scanning the rocks and woods below her for a hiding place. But it was too late.

"She's here!" a male voice shouted to her right.

She turned to see where the voice was coming from, then felt a sudden and clammy wave of terror wash over her. The man was heavyset; he wore a red bandana tied over his long black

hair and wraparound sunglasses. A green gaiter mask with an image of two sharp rows of
teeth was pulled up over his mouth and large
bulbous nose and made the lower half of his
face look like a crocodile.

God help me!

She prayed, turned and ran. But a skinny
man in a similar getup blocked her path. He
had a mustard-yellow mask that looked like a
jaguar's jaw. He lunged at her and his hands
grabbed ahold of her backpack. She wrenched
her arms free of the straps and started running
down the side of the hill.

The mud beneath her feet was slick. She
lost her footing and began to slide. Her body
slithered down the steep ground. Her hands
scraped the brush, and her elbows knocked
against stones as she struggled to stop. Finally,
her foot wedged hard against a rock. She stumbled to her feet and kept running. Dense forest
lay to her left and a long beach to her right. She
made it to the shore and ran down the beach in
the hopes she could make her way around the
shoreline back to where she'd hidden her kayak.

She didn't see the tall figure behind the
rocks until he'd leaped out at her, as if he'd
been lying in wait. He grabbed her arms and
then took hold of both her hands in one of his.

It was Anthony.

Relief filled her core.

"There are men in masks on this island, and they're hunting me," she said and glanced back toward the trees. "I think I lost them, and this cove is pretty well sheltered from view, but we've got to hide."

Anthony hesitated and looked up the hill behind her. Silence fell from the woods around them.

"I don't hear or see anyone," Anthony said and his blue eyes grew serious. "I'm sorry, Tessa, but I have to arrest you."

Arrest her?

"We don't have time for this!" Her voice rose. "I told you there are men in masks—"

"Tessa!" He cut her off. "Your accomplice tried to kill me!"

"What accomplice?" she asked. "I'm not working with anyone!"

"The man who rented the kayak for you! He had a tattoo on his wrist."

What?

"A woman rented the boat for me, not a man," she said. "A client. Well, a prospective client. It was someone on my private investigations agency's social media page."

"I want to believe you," Anthony said. "I really do. Just tell me you'll cooperate. I'll take you into custody, and we can sort it out at the station."

His free hand moved so quickly she didn't even realize what he had done until she felt the cold sting of metal against her wrists. She looked down. Anthony had handcuffed her.

"Tessa Watson," he said, "I'm arresting you on the charge of obstructing and impeding an official police investigation—"

Emotion overwhelmed reason. She wrenched away from him, turned and ran blindly down the beach, with her hands handcuffed behind her back.

"Come on, Tessa!" Anthony shouted. "Stop! We found Cassidy's body! She's dead."

She faltered a footstep and nearly fell, as though she'd taken a bullet to the back. She turned and saw the sorrow flooding his eyes, as if now that he'd started to tell her the truth, he knew he couldn't stop.

"Tess," he said. "I could get in real trouble for telling you this, but they think you killed her."

THREE

Anthony saw the future of his career flash before his eyes as he watched the color drain from Tessa's face.

"I wasn't authorized to tell you that," Anthony said. "I could face disciplinary action or even be demoted for this, but I needed to tell you."

For reasons he couldn't even begin to put into words.

"I've spent years researching her case," Tessa said. Her voice barely rose above a whisper, as if his words had physically knocked the air from her lungs. "I gathered information. I contacted police over and over again, begging them to listen to what I had to say and look for her."

"I know," he said.

"Cassidy's bracelet was found on this island," Tessa said. "I got a notification from an online auction site this morning. It led me to a pawnshop owner in Whistler who told me it had been found on this island less than twenty-four hours ago. That's why I'm here." Her lower lip trembled. "I never gave up hope she was still alive."

"Neither did I," he admitted.

Tessa's limbs shook. He ran for her, caught her around the waist and gathered her up into his arms before she could fall. She crumpled against him, and he felt the warmth of her breath against his neck.

"It's okay," he whispered. "I've got you. I'm so sorry to tell you like this, but I promise we're going to find out who did it. Now, come on. Let's get off this island."

She pulled back and looked up at him. Confusion filled her eyes, mingled with defiance. "You honestly think I killed Cassidy?"

"I never said I thought that—" he started.

"You handcuffed me!"

"You ran!"

He reached for his keys to take the cuffs off, hoping the fact he'd now told her about Cassidy would be enough to keep her from running again. But before he could get to them something rustled in the trees.

Tessa's face paled. "They've found me."

"Hang on," he said. "You were serious about the masked men?"

The full body blow was so swift and sudden that Anthony had already been knocked to the ground before he realized his attacker must have leaped on him from above. His body hit the dirt. Immediately, he reared back and pushed up with the full force of his limbs, tossing the man off him. He was heavyset with wraparound sunglasses, a red bandana tied low over long dark hair and a green gaiter mask similar to the white one worn by the man who'd shot him.

"Tessa, run!" Anthony shouted.

He barely had time to gasp for breath before a skinny man in a yellow mask rushed at him from the side. Then it was two against one, and all Anthony could do was duck, dodge, strike back and try to survive. Anthony prayed for Tessa's safety and his own. He quickly realized that neither of his attackers were trained fighters. They were both too sloppy, their punches were too wild, they rushed forward when they should've held back and hesitated when they should have struck. All of which gave him a slim advantage, but one that he would take.

He could tell a lot about a man from the way they tried to pummel him into the ground.

These men weren't hardened criminals. At least not in the obvious way that resulted in handcuffs, warrants and jail cells. The green-masked one was even pulling his punches. But he could tell they hid a kind of opportunist evil on the inside, like the type of man who claimed to care for clients while scamming them.

A well-timed elbow jab was all it took for his first attacker to call it quits. The man was panting heavily, and Anthony imagined it couldn't be easy to breathe under those masks. If only he could manage to pull one off and see who was beneath. Anthony was down to one attacker now, and while he could feel the ache of pain and fatigue slowing him he knew the man in the mask would be feeling it even more.

Then he heard Tessa scream. The blood froze in his veins. They'd gotten her.

"Get down now!" a man's voice ordered. "Or I'll hurt her!"

Anthony heard Tessa whimper and knew the man wasn't bluffing.

With one final surge of adrenaline Anthony tossed his remaining attacker off and onto the ground. Then he got to his feet and raised his hands in front of him. With the right, he held up his badge. His eyes took in the scene.

Tessa knelt down in the wet sand on the

other side of the cove. The man in the white mask who'd lodged a bullet in Anthony's chest now stood over Tessa. He had one hand wrenched cruelly around her hair. With the other he pressed a handgun to the side of her temple. Anthony had been wrong in thinking he was Tessa's accomplice. If the man was surprised to see Anthony alive, his face and eyes were so shielded that Anthony couldn't tell. The two other masked men flanked Anthony on either side, looking exhausted but ready to strike. As if on cue, both of them pulled handguns, as well.

"I don't want to hurt her," the man yelled. His mask made him look like he had fangs. "I promise I won't even lay a hand on her, if she just cooperates and comes with me."

Tears filled Tessa's eyes. But as Anthony watched she gritted her teeth, raised her chin and refused to let the tears fall.

"I'm Sergeant Anthony Jones of the RCMP Major Crimes Unit!" His voice rose clear and strong. "Let her go now!"

The man in the white mask chuckled. It was an ugly sound.

"No thank you, officer!" he said. "You're going to toss your weapon and lie facedown on the ground. You're outnumbered. Again, if you surrender now, I promise I won't hurt her and will let her live. But if you don't, you'll soon find out you don't like what I'm capable of."

Anthony was outgunned. If he fired quickly enough, he'd be able to take out one of the masked men. Maybe even two. But there was no way he'd be able to take out all three. And he wouldn't be able to help Tessa if he was dead.

Anthony's eyes locked on her face.

"Don't do it!" she called. "Don't surrender. Fight. Run. Leave me. Go find out who killed Cass. I'll be okay."

Courage and pain filled her voice. No, she wouldn't be okay. The masked man yanked her back harshly, but she didn't cry out. He could continue to fight. But at what cost? Did he really want to risk that Tessa could die because of him?

Help me, Lord, he prayed. *I need Your wisdom now more than ever. Fill me with Your courage. Empower me with Your strength.*

Then he felt peace and certainty sweep over him like a wave. Anthony knew what kind of man he was—and it wasn't the kind who ran. He dropped to his knees on the ground.

"Anthony, no!" Tessa shouted. "Don't do it! Please! Save yourself!"

"I'm sorry," he said. "I'm not running and leaving you here alone."

He pulled out his weapon and tossed it on the ground. Then he raised his hands in surrender.

Tessa watched helplessly as the masked men took Anthony's phone, wallet, keys, badge and gun. They ordered Anthony to lie facedown in the dirt and place his hands behind his head. The man in the green mask emptied her sweatshirt pockets and told her to lie down beside Anthony. She complied, and the fact her wrists were still handcuffed made her fall partially on her side, facing Anthony. The man in the green mask then handed her keys, wallet and phone, along with Anthony's, to the man in the white mask, who seemed to be in charge. She noticed none of them had her backpack, which might mean they'd tossed it somewhere.

Rain dotted the ground around them, creating ever changing patterns in the sand. When the man in the green mask had searched her, he'd missed the small LED light in her back pocket, not that she envisioned it would be much help in an escape besides temporarily blinding someone as a diversion. But he'd also missed the thin tent peg she had hidden up her sleeve, just past her elbow, and that was a proper weapon if she could just slide it down into her hands. It was a little bit longer than a straw and solid metal with a hook at one end and a sharp point at the other. But she wasn't able to get to it with her hands cuffed, and the men had taken Anthony's keys.

The three men paced in a semicircle around them.

They were arguing. Her inner investigator tried to tune out her fear and instead focus on every detail she could glean about who these men were and what they wanted—profiling them, as if they were nothing more than three suspects taped up on the evidence board in her home office.

The heavyset man in the green mask seemed particularly agitated about the fact Anthony was a cop. He kept repeating that this was supposed to be a simple kidnap job, he wasn't a bad guy and he definitely hadn't signed up to kill anyone.

The man in the yellow mask was agitated too, but like he was itching for a fight. He seemed even less prepared for whatever this was. He swore the most and had the kind of fidgety jitters of a man who was used to popping, drinking or smoking something to take the edge off. He argued that they hadn't come prepared to kidnap two people, they wouldn't be able to get two hostages onto a boat without one of them getting away and that they should just put a bullet in Anthony's head, grab her and go.

But it was the man with the white baseball hat that scared her the most. He was altogether too calm and clearly in charge. Not to mention he had the strong physical frame of someone who wouldn't be easy to either outrun or out-maneuver in a fight. He stepped away from the other two and placed a phone call. She couldn't hear a word he was saying.

"Are you okay?" Anthony asked, in a hushed whisper. "Did they hurt you?"

"I'm fine," she said. She'd been slightly banged up, but nothing compared to the blows he had just taken. She watched as the man in the white mask held the phone to his ear. There was a dark blue-black smudge of ink on his wrist, like a badly applied tattoo that had bled under the skin until it was an unrecognizable shape. Then suddenly what Anthony had told her on the beach before they'd been attacked flashed to the front of her mind. "You said that you thought I had an accomplice, with a tattoo on his wrist, who tried to kill you."

She'd dismissed that comment at the time and then been so overwhelmed by what he'd said about Cassidy that she'd almost forgotten it. But now the memory sent fresh urgency surging through her veins.

"That would be our friend in the white hat," Anthony said, answering her unspoken question. "I was trying to track down the person who stashed the kayak in the cove for you."

"And he attacked you?"

"He shot at me."

She sucked in a painful breath.

"But I'm fine," he said. He wasn't even looking at her. Instead, his gaze seemed fixed on the ground ahead of him. "It hit my bulletproof vest. And I'm still wearing it now."

Right, like that meant he'd aim there again next time.

"Plus I'm getting the impression they were not authorized to kill us," he added. "So maybe he'd been acting on instinct or the situation changed."

How could he sound so calm about this? Wasn't he scared? She was terrified.

"I told you men were chasing me," she said. "This wouldn't have happened if you'd believed me."

"This also wouldn't have happened if you'd

cooperated with me back on the mainland," he shot back. "Who are they?"

Okay, he wasn't emotionless. He was irritated and had been holding it in.

"I have no idea," she said. "I told you not to surrender to them."

"I had to," Anthony said. "It was the only way to save your life."

"I never asked you to save me."

Anthony's head turned, his eyes snapped to her face, and suddenly it was like a shield had dropped and she could finally see the depth of emotion filling his eyes. He still cared about her despite all the angry words and years of silence. And she knew in that instant that not only would he not hesitate to risk his life to save hers but that she would've done the same for him.

"I don't want to see you get hurt," she said.

His lips parted as if there were words there waiting to be spoken. Then he closed his mouth and looked away.

She closed her eyes and tried to settle her heart. If they didn't stop fighting and start figuring out how they were going to escape they were both going to die. But before she could say anything more, the masked men came to an agreement. They decided to handcuff Tessa and Anthony to each other, on the theory it would make it easier to guard them and harder for them to escape. Then they'd march them to their boat and take them to shore. They didn't discuss what would happen from there, but she knew it wouldn't be good.

One man yanked her arms around to face him, uncuffed her left hand and handcuffed it to Anthony's right. Then the men hauled them to their feet and marched them single file through the rough and untamed brush. The man with the white hat took the lead, with Anthony and Tessa and the other two men in the rear. Anthony linked his fingers through hers and squeezed her hand reassuringly.

"So, how much are they paying you to kidnap me?" Tessa asked, loudly.

"Shut up," the man in the yellow mask muttered from behind her.

"It has to be a lot," Tessa went on, "because you'll have to split it three ways. Does that mean that he or she has really deep pockets? Or are you guys doing all this for chump change?"

"Shut it!" the yellow-masked man snapped, following it up with a swear word. He shoved her hard in the shoulder, and she would've fallen if it hadn't been for Anthony's strong grip holding her fast. The sound of Anthony's keys jangled in the man's sweatshirt pocket. So that's where they were.

They walked forward in silence, picking their way over the inhospitable terrain. Her mind whirled. They had to escape before their kidnappers had them in the boat. Once they were out on the water there'd be no way to escape, and there was no knowing who or what would be waiting for them on the shore. A narrow cove lay ahead through the trees with a small metal boat. It had a motor in the back, two wooden plank benches for seats and clearly hadn't been meant for five adult-sized people. The propeller was pulled up, and the water was so shallow they'd have to paddle out a ways before putting it in the water. They started toward it.

She took a step forward and pretended to stumble against Anthony. Her body hit his back. Her face fell against his ear.

"When we're in the boat, I'm going to cause a distraction and grab your keys from him," she whispered, nodding toward the man who'd taken them.

Anthony's head shook.

"Don't," Anthony whispered. "I think I can get through to the one in the green mask."

He honestly thought he could turn a criminal in the middle of a kidnapping and convince the guy to help them? Was he kidding her with this? A small voice inside her told her to trust him. But how could she when they actually had an opportunity to escape?

"Keep walking!" the man in the yellow mask snapped. "Just because I can't kill you doesn't mean I won't hurt you."

She complied and they kept walking. They reached the waterside. The men pushed the boat off the shore and ordered them to get inside. The man in the white hat sat in the bow and pointed his gun at them. Anthony and Tessa sat on the middle seat. The heavy-set one knelt in front of them, grabbed a paddle and started pushing them out toward the deeper water. The skinny one who had Anthony's keys in his pocket crouched behind them and did the same.

The rain grew heavier. The wind became wilder. The cove was narrow, and they struggled to turn the boat around to face the open water. They'd have to paddle out a ways before they could safely drop the motor into the water. She watched the gray-green water as they maneuvered until they'd reached a depth of five or six feet. Tessa waited until she heard the sound of the propeller splashing into the water, followed by the metallic scraping of the man behind her yanking the chain to start the engine. She spun back, slid the tent peg from her sleeve into her fingers and quickly jabbed him in the leg just as the motor caught. The boat shot forward.

He swore and jolted in shock. "I think I got stung by something!"

The keys fell from his pocket. She grabbed for them and turned back, hoping nobody noticed, only to see one of their other kidnappers swing a paddle around toward her like a club.

Anthony raised his free arm and blocked the blow. The boat swung wildly.

Tessa lost her footing and fell over the side of the boat, dragging Anthony into the water with her.

FOUR

She hit the water and struggled toward the surface, only to be dragged back down by the force of Anthony's body tumbling into the water on top of her. The air was knocked from her lungs. She felt her body hit the muddy ground. She gripped the keys tightly and tried to swim, but instead her left arm pulled against the handcuff that linked her arm to Anthony's, as if thrashing hard enough would allow her to break free. She thought she was going to drown.

Then she felt Anthony wrap his strong arm around her waist. He picked her up, pulled her out of the water and ran for the shore, carrying her against his chest like an unwieldy sack of potatoes. Behind her she could hear their kidnappers shouting and scrambling as they struggled to turn around to come after them. The fact she'd timed her ungraceful escape for when the boat had shot forward meant they'd need a few minutes or more to stop moving and then maneuver the boat back around. That would buy her and Anthony a small window of time to get away. But not much.

Anthony stumbled up onto the shore and carried her up past the rocks. She coughed and tried to regain her breath. "Put me down."

He set her down so quickly she nearly fell.

"What were you thinking, Tessa?" he demanded. Water streamed down the lines of his face. "You could've killed us!"

"I saved us!" she said. She waved his key chain. "I got your keys. So we can get these handcuffs off."

They weren't going to get far handcuffed together. A bullet flew across the water and struck the ground to their right, sending dirt flying. They ran for the shelter of the nearby rocks and crouched down low. The masked men had cut the engine and were using the paddles to try to turn around.

"I thought they weren't supposed to shoot us!" she said.

"No, they weren't supposed to kill us," Anthony said. "I think the guy in the yellow mask has gone rogue, and white-mask would rather have us wounded than escape." And he'd believed he'd have been able to turn the guy in the green mask, based on a two-minute interaction. Anthony's right hand grabbed ahold of her forearm, and the handcuffs jingled as the chain fell between them. "Come on. My boat's moored down on a beach not far from where we ran into each other."

He tugged her back toward the area they'd come from. But she dug her heels and pulled him in the opposite direction.

"No," she said. "There's not a lot of cover that way. We're safer heading for the caves and taking the underground tunnels. Trust me."

A second bullet whizzed by. The sounds of the motor and shouting were drawing closer. She glanced back over her shoulder. The masked men had managed to turn the boat around and were heading back their way.

"Fine," he said. "Just don't try anything."

They were stuck on an island, handcuffed to each other and being chased by criminals. What could he possibly think she was about to try?

His fingers slipped to hers. Tessa and Anthony ran, hand in hand, pressing through the thick trees and scrambling up the slippery rocks toward the northernmost tip of the island. Within moments she'd lost sight of the men pursuing them in the dense foliage, but she could hear the sound of them crashing through the woods after them. Her heart pounded through her chest. Her lungs ached with every breath. But she didn't let her pace slow and matched Anthony step for step.

Suddenly the trees broke and a wall of rock stood before them, stretching up over thirty feet above her head. Anthony sucked in a sharp breath as he scanned the wall for hand and footholds, and she realized that although he didn't let it show he was probably as winded as she was. His bulletproof vest had to weigh at least twenty pounds.

"You've got to be kidding me," Anthony said.

She had to admit the climb looked a lot easier on her aerial map.

"Well, when I first planned this route, I wasn't planning on being handcuffed to anyone," she said.

He snorted. Hang on. Had she really just made him laugh?

Anthony glanced behind them, as if judging how close their pursuers were and debating whether they had time to stop and unlock the handcuffs.

She pulled Anthony's key ring out of her

pocket and shoved the handcuff key into the lock. It wouldn't turn. "It's stuck!"

"Stop or you'll jam it!" Anthony said. "They're really finicky, and they break far more often than you'd think."

She tried to yank the key back out of the lock, but it wouldn't budge. It was wedged in.

"Here let me handle it!" Anthony pushed her hand away and yanked the key out of the lock. "Key's bent. I can fix it, but not right this second." Was he implying she'd bent it? "Good news is it's not the hardest climb, except that we're kind of stuck together for now."

That was one way to put it. As long as their hands were cuffed, they wouldn't be able to get more than a few feet apart. Anthony braced his right leg against the rock. "You go first. I'll give you a step up. Then I'll follow right behind you."

She accepted the offer, stepped one foot up on to his knee and planted the other on the rock. They started to climb in tandem. It was slow going, painstaking and methodical as her eyes scanned the rocks and sought out the next grip, one step at a time. It didn't help that Anthony was constantly in her ear, telling her how to proceed and where to grab, even though she could tell he was only trying to be helpful.

She reached the top first, climbed over the edge and looked back.

Anthony's right arm was fully extended above his head, thanks to still being handcuffed to hers. His fingertips pressed into the rock face at the very edge of the cliff as he struggled to get his grip. She dropped onto her stomach and reached both hands down toward him.

"Here," she said. "Grab my hands, and I'll help pull you up."

"No," he said. "I've got it. Last thing I want is to pull you over the edge."

He reached past her and grabbed ahold of a small patch of crabgrass growing straight out of the rock. Blades of grass tore in his fingers, but he made it up high enough to slide his elbows over the ledge and haul himself over.

She heard the clink of something metal hitting the rocks. The keys had fallen out of Anthony's pocket and onto a ledge beside him. She snatched them up before they could tumble over the edge and shoved them deep inside her sweatshirt.

They both climbed to their feet and found themselves on another long slab of uneven gray rock that spread out beneath their feet in both directions. Tessa couldn't see her attackers through the trees but she could hear them coming and watched the branches sway as they grew closer.

"This way." She gestured to their left, and they started jogging. "Okay, so the plan is to run to the mouth of the caves, go through the underground tunnels and climb up a well-like sinkhole near my campsite, find my backpack and escape the island."

"We don't want to waste time searching for your bag," he started.

"Either way, the underground tunnels are our best way off this island."

But despite her hopes their kidnappers hadn't tried to climb up the rocks after them, it sounded like the three masked men were now running parallel to them through the trees, as if trying to get ahead of Tessa and Anthony and cut them off.

Then the trees broke below them and she finally saw the men pursuing her. She gasped. Weeks ago she'd looked out her second-story window to see a shadowy figure standing below her on her lawn—they were that close now.

"There they are!" the man in the yellow wildcat mask shouted. He took aim and fired. A bullet flew up the rock face toward them and struck the ground near their feet.

The man in the white mask started to climb up toward them. The man in the yellow mask fired again. The third man ran ahead, as if trying to find another way up.

Her plan wasn't going to work. They needed a new way to escape and fast.

"Come on!" she said. "There's another way to get inside the caves!"

She grabbed Anthony's hand and pulled him back the way they came. They passed the spot where they'd climbed upland and kept running. She could see the rock face disappearing ahead of them, leaving nothing but gray sky and dark green water beyond. Footsteps sounded behind them. At least one of the men had made it up. Then she heard Anthony praying out loud, asking God to save them both. She prayed too.

Lord, please answer Anthony's prayers. He may not be the man I'd have chosen to be stuck with at a moment like this. But he's the one You've brought to me now. Help me to trust in You and in him. And help Anthony to trust in me.

The edge of the rock loomed closer, jutting out like a cliff over the water.

"Tessa!" he shouted. "We're going to run right off the edge!"

She could feel Anthony's footsteps beginning to slow. But she tightened her grip of his hand. She'd never liked heights, let alone jumping from them, but it beat getting shot.

"I know!" she shouted. "Trust me! We need to get to the very tip and jump out as far as we can, otherwise we'll hit the rocks!"

A garbled syllable slipped from Anthony's lips, like he'd just barely stopped himself from arguing.

The rock face grew closer. Twenty feet, then fifteen feet, then ten. If they didn't leap out far enough they'd dash themselves against the sharp rocks below.

What would happen when she jumped? Would he hesitate? Would he falter? Or would he trust her and jump too?

Then it was too late to stop. The ground had run out beneath their feet. Her foot pushed off from the edge of the rock, and she leaped.

Anthony leaped out as far as he could, pushing through the wall of logic and doubt telling him not to. Then he and Tessa were in free fall. Their fingers slipped away from each other's as they plummeted through the air toward the rocks and sea below. He hit the water and went under. It was deeper than he expected, and colder too, with a current that threatened to drag him under.

Tessa grabbed his hand again and guided him as they swam for the surface. Their heads broke through. He looked around and at first saw nothing but jagged gray rocks towering around them on all sides.

"This way," Tessa said.

Then he saw it. There was a gap in the rocks, about as wide as his first car and barely two-thirds its height. They swam for it as he heard the voice of their would-be kidnappers floating down from somewhere above them. Then he and Tessa reached the rock side, hauled themselves up and slid through the opening. A deep limestone cave lay ahead of him, spreading out into the darkness. The air was cold and damp around them. For a moment he lay there on his back inside the cave with Tessa by his side, fighting to slow his breath and calm his racing heartbeat.

Thank. You. Lord.

Then the faint hint of rain that had been drizzling on and off ever since they'd first been taken hostage on the beach suddenly broke in earnest, sending a rush of water falling down outside the entrance of their hiding place. His heart rate slowed, and his eyes adjusted to the low light around them.

Tessa sat up slowly and so did he. Her lips parted as if she was about to say something. Instead, she closed them again, and her eyes seemed to lock on his face. Her normally frizzy hair lay in long dark curls against her cheeks. Her hazel eyes were large in the dim light. Something stirred inside his chest like the echo of a feeling he hadn't known in a very long time.

For years, Tessa Watson had lurked like a shadow on the edges of his memory. Had he been glad the relationship was over? Yes, because clearly they'd been too different to have any real future together. But he'd never forgotten her, never stopped wondering how she was or made it through a full day without feeling the urge to just give in and type her name into a search engine, just to see her face. As someone who'd interrogated hundreds of suspects, he knew better than most that memories lie and the human brain tricks people into thinking things were better than they actually were.

But not his memory of Tessa. Sure, she was every bit as aggravating as he remembered, with the same knack for getting on his nerves. But she was stronger too, smarter and braver, filled with more courage and optimism.

Not to mention she was also far more beautiful.

"Here's hoping that's the last time I ever have to jump off something that tall," she said.

Tessa leaned toward him. He felt the fingers of her free hand brush along the palm of the hand still cuffed to hers. The space between them shrink. And a terrifying thought crossed his mind. Was Tessa about to kiss him? If she did, would he kiss her back?

Then he heard the metallic jingle of his keys in the darkness and realized she was trying to unlock their hands.

"Here, let me," he said and pulled his keychain from her fingers. "Like I said there is a trick to it. You don't want to know how many times it takes three different officers to get one suspect's handcuffs off."

She let him take her hand in his. He felt for the key, carefully pressed it against the stone to straighten it, and slid it into the lock. He jiggled it back and forth for a long moment until finally there was a metallic clink, and the cuffs opened.

"Thank you." Her voice came out in a rush. "No offense, but I can't tell you how happy I am to have both my hands back again."

"I want you to take my bulletproof vest," he said. "In case they start shooting at us again."

"No," she said. "Don't. I'm half your size. It's way too big for me. It'll only swing around and slow me down."

No, he wasn't twice her size. More like one and a half, tops. But she was right that the bulletproof vest was way too big for her, and if they had to run or swim again, that might be even more dangerous than not wearing one at all.

"Besides," she said. "I like knowing you're safe."

She reached around into her back pocket and pulled out something so small he couldn't make out what it was. She flipped her thumb over it, and he watched as a small round light, about the size of a 'toonie' two-dollar coin, flickered to life. The space around them was illuminated by a warm yellow glow, enveloping them both.

"Got any more tricks up your sleeve?" he asked.

"Not on me, no," she said. "But I do have a bunch of camping stuff back where I set up base when I first arrived."

"My boss, Chief Superintendent Zablocie, told me there's a constable with the Emergency

Response Team who has a cottage near Princess," Anthony said. "He offered to call him in for me. I'd turned him down. I wish I hadn't."

"Well, maybe someone will get worried when you don't call in and send him here after us," she said.

Hopefully his sister would. He had promised her that he'd be in touch. He wondered if anyone would call the police if Tessa disappeared, then remembered she hadn't spoken to her parents in years. Not that he had any idea why.

Tessa frowned.

"These guys who are after us aren't professionals," she said. "They don't care about covering their tracks, and they're not really cooperating with each other. There's no sense of teamwork between them. Based on their actions I would've assumed they're desperate, but they didn't sound that way when they were arguing. They sounded more angry and resentful. Like they'd been sent to get me by someone and resented it."

He felt his eyes widen. "You picked up on all that?"

Obviously, he had too. But while she talked as if they were all the same, in his estimation the three men were three completely different individuals—the man who was in charge but wanted to believe he was "hands off," the one who was there reluctantly and trying to tell himself no one would get hurt and the loose cannon who was more than happy to go rogue.

"I've had stalkers on and off for years, Anthony," she said. "Comes with the territory of being a private investigator."

Something lurched in his chest.

"I'm so sorry," he said. "I wish I'd known. I'd have done something."

"The average police response time in Vancouver is eight minutes and forty-three seconds," she said, with a dry tone to imply that being stalked never really bothered her, despite a slight tremor in her voice that made it very obvious it had. "As I'm sure you know, in Canada, you can't get a restraining order against someone you're not in some kind of a relationship with. That leaves a lesser kind of protection order called 'a peace bond,' but those require knowing the person's name, address and contact details. Besides, they expire after a year."

So, she'd tried to get one, he imagined. More than once probably and failed.

"Besides," she added softly, "I know how to take care of myself."

"I know," he said. "I just wish I'd been there

to help you." She pressed her lips together and didn't answer. He peered into the darkness. "How deep do these caves go? I'm hoping that there's another exit somewhere you know about, and we're not going to have to swim for it."

"I'm honestly not sure if they meet the definition of karst caves or not," she said, "but based on the maps and satellite footage I was able to gather, there's a long underground tunnel with a few different branches that's essentially a dried-out river, along with some sinkhole shafts, like wells, that shouldn't be too hard to climb up."

"And it's all dry?" Anthony said.

"I believe so," she said.

"But it could flood if the rain keeps on like this."

"Yup," she nodded.

Okay, so they were safe and dry for now, but then what? If they jumped out into the storm and started swimming for it, they could get picked off by any of the kidnappers who were waiting for them out there. But if they ran through the caves and climbed out, they could run straight into the masked men that way too.

He sat cross-legged and leaned back against the wall while she did the same against the opposite one, and they both turned their faces to look out at where the rain fell like a waterfall across the opening of the cave.

"Hopefully," he said, "if we give it a few minutes they'll give up and leave. Then we can head for my boat. It's not much bigger than theirs, but it's fast and can fit two people, which is more than I can say for your kayak."

"We should head back to my camp first and get supplies," she said, "especially as we don't know if they tried to sabotage your boat. I've got things like duct tape and tarps we can use to do an emergency patch job if we need to."

Instinctively he opened his mouth to argue, before realizing neither option was wrong. Had he always been this argumentative? Or did she just bring it out in him?

"I have a spare cell phone in my truck," he said. "I can use it to call my boss as soon as we get out of here. My laptop's in my truck too."

"My laptop is back at the hotel," she said.

She pressed her lips together. He could tell a question was weighing on her mind.

"You mentioned that you're in Crisis Negotiation," she said. "If I hadn't grabbed the keys and we'd made a run for it, do you honestly think you could've convinced the man in the green mask to just hand you his gun and help us?"

"Like my childhood hero, General Alberto McClean?" he asked, with a hint of a smile. "I honestly don't know. I had a hunch, but who knows."

She ran both hands through her wet hair and let the strands fall through her fingers.

"All right, well, let's do a recap," she added, "because I don't know about you, but I feel like I missed half of what you were trying to tell me when we were running for our lives."

He chuckled, despite himself.

"Fair enough," he said. "Do you wanna go first?"

"All right," she said. "So, as you know, I'm a private investigator. Back in university, I was getting a general arts and sciences degree, studying a little bit of everything. Psychology, sociology, research skills, forensics—a total grab bag of stuff. Then a girl in my dorm was hacked by someone pretending to be her and police claimed they didn't have enough evidence to take action. And maybe it was because of what happened to Cassidy, I got really worked up about that and took it upon myself to get the evidence she needed."

That was further back than he'd been expecting. But it was a good place to start.

"And did you?" he asked.

"I did," she said with a slightly sad smile. "She got a 'peace bond' aka a protective order against him."

Anthony stopped himself from pointing out that as he was an RCMP officer she didn't need to keep explaining official terminology to him. He assumed she was just used to explaining things to clients.

"Wow," he said. "Congratulations."

"Thanks," she said. "Anyway, the rest is history. I took the required private investigator course and became licensed in the province of British Columbia. I'm now licensed in Alberta, as well."

"Your parents must've been proud," he said.

She turned and looked out at the rain.

"You know as well as anyone that they've always had pretty rigid ideas about how things should be done," she said. "They didn't understand why I was dropping out of school to start my own business and were a bit too concerned about making sure I knew what I was doing. Like they'd double-check I was scrupulous about following the law, stuff like that. Then a few years later I discovered a thing, while

I was researching something, and it drove a pretty big wedge between us."

"Do you want to talk about it?" he asked.

"No, not really," she said. "Anyway, I got my license and started investigating crimes. My main focus at the time was trying to find out what had happened to Cassidy. She'd been gone maybe two years by this point, and the trail had gone cold. Finding her became my obsession. Since then I've probably gathered enough research on the case for books, a full-length documentary and a twelve-hour podcast, and that wouldn't even begin to scrape the surface." She sighed. "Then this morning, around eight thirty, my phone went off with an email and text telling me that Cassidy's bracelet has been posted on an online auction site."

"How did it know to contact you?" he asked.

"I set up alerts on multiple sites," she said. "No different than people setting up alerts to tell them if someone, somewhere in the world puts a vintage comic book or antique figurine up for sale. Online auctions rely on them."

He felt his brow crease. "I'm guessing you also set up news alerts to let you know any time a body matching Cassidy's description was found?"

She nodded. "Of course. Why?"

"Because last I heard my boss wasn't going public with the news she'd been found until four o'clock this afternoon," he said. He glanced at his watch, thankful it was still running. It was just after one. "Anyway, go ahead and finish your story."

"It's been twelve years since Cassidy walked out of that bar with a stranger and was never seen again," Tessa said, "and eight years since any new evidence has shown up in Cassidy's case. Then suddenly today a pawnshop in Whistler has her bracelet."

"You sound suspicious," he said.

"Well, I wasn't suspicious this morning," she said. "But now, considering everything that's happened so far today..." Her words trailed off. Then to his surprise, she laughed. It was a beautiful sound. "All right, I can be a big enough person to admit it. I think I might've been set up."

"I can't believe you're laughing about it," he said.

"I find laughing at my mistakes a lot more helpful these days than getting angry about them," she said. "The man at the pawnshop in Whistler told me I wasn't the only person interested and that he'd only hold it for two hours, which didn't give me a lot of time. So I jumped in my car and went."

"Hold up." He held up his hand. "That doesn't explain why you brought a wig and camping gear with you."

"I always keep some basic supplies with me in my trunk," she said, "because I never know when I'm going to suddenly be called on a job. I always have multiple cases going at a time, most of which are either missing people or victims of what you cops call 'intimate partner violence,' which thankfully law enforcement has now expanded to include both actual domestic relationships and those one-sided obsessions that only exist in the perpetrator's head."

"And those cases might mean staking out the same person for several days in several different disguises?" he asked.

"Right."

"But then why run from the police?" he asked.

"Because, like I told you, they could hold me for twenty-four hours without pressing charges or even telling me why I'm being held!" Her voice rose. "This isn't my first rodeo, cowboy. I've been picked up before because some person I was targeting had filed a bogus complaint against me and waited hours and hours for police to finally admit it was nonsense and let me go. I seem to remember you getting pretty irritated that one time you took your car in for repairs at nine thirty in the morning, and the mechanic said you'd be out of there by ten. When they still had your car at noon you were pacing around like a caged tiger."

He bristled. "That's not the same thing."

"No," she said, "because then you're able to step outside or get a drink without permission."

He gritted his teeth and prayed for grace. The uneasy truce they'd struck between them was only temporary. He still had three hours before the deadline Zablocie had given him to bring her in for questioning, and once they got back to Princess it would be a two-hour drive to the closest RCMP detachment.

"I'm not saying I agree with you," Anthony said, "but I can see where you're coming from."

"I'll take it," she said. "Anyway, you know my story after that. I got to the pawnshop and got ahold of the bracelet. He told me it was found here on the island in the past twenty-four hours, so I came here, got attacked and ran into you."

"Wait, go back a step," he said. "How did

our friend in the white mask end up renting a kayak for you and stashing it in a cove?"

"As I told you before, I have a private social media group for current, future and prospective clients," she said and her face darkened. "I posted something there about needing a boat. A woman replied saying she ran a boating company and would leave a kayak in the cove for me. Only, I'm guessing now it was a dummy account set up by whoever is behind this. Which makes me wonder just how many of my prospective clients are fakes or trolls. If we could get online we might be able to trace who's behind it. But either way, it's possible that someone has had me in their sights for a long time." She planted her feet on the ground, pulled her knees up in front of her and rested her arms on them. "Now it's your turn. What's your story?"

"There's not much to tell—"

"I don't believe you."

"I'm with the Unsolved Homicide Unit of the RCMP Major Crimes Unit."

"A unit of a unit," she interrupted again, this time with a smile.

"I didn't name them," he said. How was she managing to smile despite everything that was happening? And how was she making him smile. as well? "We got a call this morning from a construction crew at the cottage where Cassidy disappeared. They found her buried on the property. It took a couple of hours to get a positive ID, but the letter you'd written to Cassidy when you found out she'd gone back to Kevin was on her body, which immediately made you a person of interest. CSIs haven't managed to piece the whole thing together, but under the circumstances it sounded like motive."

"To be honest," she said, and the smile disappeared from her face again, "I can't even remember what I said. She'd blocked me on both her phone and computer, and I was so upset I sent her a long, handwritten letter by actual snail mail. I can't tell you how much I wish I hadn't done it. That's the kind of thing stalkers do, Anthony. Since then I've investigated enough cases to know how scary it is to get a handwritten letter from someone you've tried to block. It's the biggest regret of my life."

Something inside him wanted to reach across the gap between them, wrap her in his arms and reassure her that everyone did stupid things they regretted. But instead, he caught himself and held back.

"Well, you always were pretty hard on yourself," he said. "Two officers were dispatched to bring you in for questioning and when you declined their offer, my boss, Chief Superintendent Wade Zablocie, was ready to issue a warrant for your arrest immediately. I talked him into giving me until four o'clock. I figured that once I got you alone and talked to you, I'd be able to convince you."

"You also thought you'd be able to talk the man in the green mask into letting us go," she reminded him. He wasn't sure by her tone if she believed he could've or not. "I would've thought there was some rule against sending you to bring me in considering we used to have a relationship."

Heat rose in the back of his neck, and he ran one hand over it.

"Sending me to bring you in isn't against regulations," he said. "It's just ill-advised. But I've built up a pretty good reputation over the course of my career for getting stuff done. I've never lost a case or failed to bring in a target before. I actually teach interrogation techniques. My boss was about to blast your name all over the national news calling you a murder suspect. But when I stuck my neck out and convinced him that our best chance of success of solving the crime was to have me come in personally, he listened."

"And what happens if you don't bring me in?" she asked.

"He'll put your name out on blast," he said. "Every cop in the country will be on the look-out to arrest you, and since you have a history of running you won't be let out on bail."

"I mean what will happen to *you*?"

"I don't know," he admitted.

She didn't respond and neither did he, and for a long moment her eyes searched his face, as if looking for something she'd lost long ago. Then she glanced away.

Lord, please help me get through to Tessa. It's like there's this pain behind her eyes that's so very deep. I know that You love her. I know that You want the best for her. Help me be the person she needs me to be right now.

He took a deep breath.

"Look," he said. "For whatever it's worth, I've been praying constantly all day today. I know the way your parents talked about God never sat right with you, or with me either, for that matter. But at the risk of sounding like a cliché, I genuinely believe that God loves you and wants what's best for you, including solving what happened to Cassidy."

"That sounds exactly like something you'd say." She smiled faintly. "Glad to see some things haven't changed."

The sound of a boat motor cut through the pouring rain. He crouched forward and looked out through the gap. A sleek motorboat with its canvas top up came into view. The man in the yellow mask was at the helm. It inched slowly past their entrance and then disappeared from view.

"Looks like they're patrolling the island looking for us," Tessa said.

"It's worse than that," Anthony said. "That's my boat."

FIVE

"This means they've stolen my boat," Anthony added. She watched as he winced like he was in pain. "So much for making our way to my boat and escaping the island that way." He blew out a long breath, as if searching for words. "Hopefully we still have your kayak and can find a makeshift way to turn it into a raft big enough to fit us both. You have a tarp and duct tape. I'm guessing you also have an air mattress?"

"I do," she said.

A loud burst of thunder drowned out her voice before she could say anything more. The rain grew heavier until it kicked up spray as it hit the water. Tessa closed her eyes. She could feel frustration building inside her and mounting toward a pitch that threatened to overcome her logic.

Whoever had killed Cassidy hadn't just

taken her life, it seemed that they'd also planned to make Tessa their scapegoat if the crimes had ever come to light. Who knew how long they'd been holding on to Cassidy's bracelet, like some trophy, waiting to lure Tessa into danger the day Cassidy's body was discovered. And if they had gotten their hands on her, then what? Would they have killed her too? Used her to cover up the crime in some way? Forced her to confess to the crimes or help them frame someone else?

She could feel her mind tumbling down a rabbit hole of questions she couldn't answer and fears she couldn't quell. Anxiety overwhelmed her, tasting like acid in her mouth and pressing on her lungs until she struggled to breathe.

Then she heard the squeak of Anthony's rubber soles on the rock and felt his hands gently brush her forearms.

"Hey," he said. "It's okay. We're going to get out of this. I promise."

She opened her eyes to see Anthony crouching in front of her.

"Your boat is gone, and whoever's after us has been planning this for years," she said.

Anthony rocked back on his heels, but still the gentle touch of his fingertips lingered.

"I know," he said. "But I promise you we're going to get out of this alive and figure out who killed Cassidy."

Help me, Lord. I want to believe him. I want to have hope. But it feels like my insides are drowning.

"You look angry," he said gently. "Are you angry at me?"

Was she?

"No," she said. "I don't know. Maybe. I'm terrified and overwhelmed. And yes, I think I'm angry. It's hard to explain. It's like whenever I think about what happened to Cassidy there's this tangled mass of feelings inside me, all hissing like poisonous snakes, and I can't even figure out where one feeling ends and another begins."

He didn't answer. He just nodded. And she realized for all the time she'd spent trying to solve the case, she'd never actually sat with anyone and tried to unpack the feelings behind it all.

"I am angry at the five other camp counselors she was on vacation with the day she disappeared," Tessa said. "Katie Masters, Drew Roberts, Cole Rook, Lewis Fowler and Tom Groff all went to that cottage together for the weekend. They all went drinking underage in

Whistler together. None of them tried to stop Cassidy from leaving that bar with a stranger or even gave a coherent description to police. Instead, they all told police they'd barely known her and didn't even report her missing until noon the next day. Of course, I still suspect Kevin had something to do with it, but the facts of the case remain that she left the bar with an unknown man who didn't fit Kevin's description."

And wanting someone to be guilty, or even suspecting they were, didn't make it so.

"Obviously, I'm angry at whoever took her life," she went on, "and somehow knowing her body was found back at the cottage and that my letter was found on the body makes it even worse. Because now we know the killer's cover-up was intentional. He took her wallet and phone, so he could plant a false trail to make it look like she was skipping all over British Columbia and Alberta, but leaves that letter on her body? That's planning. That's evil. I'm also furious at every police officer who was fooled by this and assumed she was just some runaway teen. I'm livid at the media for playing into that narrative, dredging up all her baggage and calling her troubled because she wasn't a perfect, squeaky-clean victim."

She half expected him to argue. But again, all he did was nod. Tessa took a deep breath and let it out slowly.

"It makes our job as police harder when the public and media pick and choose which victims to have sympathy for," he admitted, "and which searches they're willing to put manpower into helping us with."

Somehow it helped to hear him say it. For years her ability to harness her anger and frustration had served her well. She hadn't realized how good it would feel to share her burdens with somebody else.

"Well, that's where people like me come in," she said, "to provide that extra help." She took in another even longer breath, held it for a second and then blew it out. "And yes, I'm angry at you and me both. If you hadn't called my folks from the hospital, I wouldn't have been banned from going to camp, and I might've been there and stopped her from getting hurt. Instead, she died thinking I hated her."

Hot tears swam to the edges of her eyes. She blinked hard and felt one slip down her cheek.

"I'm sorry," Anthony said. He leaned forward and she felt his thumb brush the tear from her face. "For what it's worth, I think Cassidy knew you loved her and that you only sent her that letter because you were worried about her."

"I just wish she'd never gone back to Kevin," Tessa said, "or left the bar with a stranger that night."

"Me too."

She watched as Anthony closed his eyes, and what looked like a silent prayer crossed his lips, asking for guidance. Then he opened his eyes, stood and reached for her hand.

"I vote we start walking," he said, "and find another way out of here."

"Agreed."

She reached up her hand toward his, and he clasped it and pulled her to her feet. His hand lingered in hers.

"I also suggest that while we walk, we use this time to solve her murder," he said.

"You're kidding, right?" Cassidy's disappearance had been unsolved for twelve years, and he thought they'd be able to solve it while stuck underground in some caves?

"Not in the slightest," he said with a grin that was both determined and infectious. "I'm a sergeant with the Unsolved Homicide Unit. You're the world's utmost expert on the Cassidy Chase case. We've come face-to-face with three suspects. If anyone has the combined ability to solve this crime it's us."

Was this his way to distract her mind, help her stay calm and keep her from panicking? Or was he thinking about how he was going to bring her in for questioning, and he saw this as some kind of opportunity to preinterview her to find out what she knew? Or, after all this time, did he still understand her so well that he figured this was all she would be thinking about anyway and was genuinely interested in her opinion?

Slowly, they started making their way through the tunnel and deeper into the caves. She went first, picking her way over the uneven rocky ground and feeling her way along the cave walls with her hands, while Anthony was one step behind her, holding up the flashlight so it shone down on them both. Soon the faint gray light of the world behind them disappeared from view. But the sound of the rain lingered around them like white noise.

"I think the light's dimmer than it was," Anthony said.

"Me too," she admitted. "I don't know how much longer it's going to last."

"What can you tell me about Cassidy's five friends?" he asked.

"I don't think you could really classify them as friends so much as colleagues," Tessa said. "She'd only been working with them for about three weeks by that point. They all happened to have the same weekend off and Katie had rented a cabin and was looking for people to go in on the cost with."

"And who's Katie?"

"Katie Masters was eighteen at the time of Cassidy's disappearance," Tessa said. "Although she lied about her age to rent the cottage. She taught drama and was in the same cabin as Cassidy."

"And where is she now?"

"In Nova Scotia," Tessa said. "With two kids and married to her high school sweetheart. He's a software engineer and threatened to get a restraining order against me if I kept trying to question his wife."

"Do you think she knew anything she didn't tell police?" Anthony asked.

"I do," she said. "I think they all do. Drew Roberts was a junior counselor, also in the drama program. He was younger than the rest of them, and had just barely turned sixteen. He made it as an actor for a while, before he got into some minor trouble and was fired. Drew then tried to get into law enforcement, flunking out of that and becoming a security guard. Lewis Fowler works at his uncle's car dealership and has been in trouble with the police a few times, mostly for drug stuff, fighting and theft, but never anything that stuck. He was eighteen when Cassidy disappeared and worked in the kitchen. Cole Rook is a defense lawyer who specializes in getting drunk drivers and domestic abusers out of trouble. He was a sports instructor then. So was Tom Groff. They were both nineteen. Last I heard, Tom was working in the kitchen of a cruise ship."

She paused for a long moment.

"Those are the five people she was actually with that day," she added. "But of course, I can't forget Kevin, her on-again, off-again boyfriend, even though there's no evidence he was there at the time and he's not who Cassidy left the bar with. Kevin Scotch-Simmonds was in his midtwenties then so he's in his late thirties now. He's still the son of Canada's second-largest grocery store chain owner and has an undefined management job at the company. But unlike his brother and parents, he doesn't appear on the cookie boxes or on marketing materials. He also has an alibi for the night Cassidy disappeared and no witnesses put him there at the time. But he has money, and you'd be surprised what people can pay other people to do."

She'd been told more than once that the only reason she couldn't shake his name from her mind was the fact she had a personal vendetta against him. Pursuing him was following her own resentments and anger—not facts.

"Not a bad summary," Anthony said.

"But the first pings that police got on both Cassidy's cell phone and debit card happened less than two hours after Cole, Drew, Tom, Katie and Lewis left the bar," she added. "And not long afterward Cassidy's belongings were traveling south of Whistler. If any of them had hurt Cassidy they'd have had very little time to leave the bar, get her, go back to the cottage, kill her and drive south immediately to start planting evidence that she'd run. The timing is so tight it's almost impossible. Especially if none of this had been planned in advance."

The tunnel grew narrower. The walls pressed in around them.

"Is it true that the police never managed to get much out of any of them?" she asked. "And that what they did get was contradictory?"

He paused, as if he was debating whether or not he could answer that question.

"I think that's fair to say," he said finally. "They all generally agreed on what time they entered the bar that night and that they all left together about an hour after Cassidy did. That was also confirmed by both security and multiple witnesses. What do you remember about the guy she left the bar with?" he asked.

"He was about six foot five with dark curly hair, and a red, white and green hoodie pulled up over his head," she said. "The Italian junior roller-ski team was in Whistler that weekend practicing at Olympic Park. It was assumed the unknown guy was one of them, except all members of the team were on the bus and accounted for less than twenty minutes later. Videos and pictures taken from the bus and posted online back that up, and they were all scanned in by passport control in Vancouver less than three hours later. None of them had time to take Cassidy back to the cottage, kill her, bury her body and get back to the bus on time."

"And no motive," Anthony said.

Then a shaft of light pierced the darkness ahead. It was a sinkhole, about six feet across and two stories tall. They stood side by side underneath it and looked up into the rain as it poured down on their faces. The walls looked so slick she wasn't even sure they'd be able to climb up it.

"What do you think?" Anthony asked. "It doesn't look all that safe. Do you think we'll find a better way out?"

"I think we should try," she said.

They kept walking. Her mind spun. She wasn't sure what the point of reviewing the case like this was. They were no closer to finding an answer to Cassidy's disappearance or a way out.

"You mentioned Kevin," Anthony said, after a long moment.

"I did," she said. "But again there's no evidence he was there that night. Several people Cassidy worked with said they were broken up again at the time she disappeared. The one time he tried to visit her at camp, she was away on a canoe trip, and he was turned away at the gate by security. Not a single witness places him anywhere near Whistler that night. And he's only five foot eleven and blond, so it definitely wasn't him in the hoodie who she left the bar with."

"Plus he has an alibi placing him in Victoria that night," Anthony added.

"From his brother and father," Tessa said, "both of whom have their faces on Scotch-

Simmonds family pasta sauce and ice cream cartons, and plenty of reason to lie for him."

"Maybe it's not Kevin but another guy like him," Anthony said. "A lot of people who escape abusive relationships fall into the same pattern with somebody else."

She stopped walking so suddenly she felt Anthony bump into her. Her back bristled. She turned around to face him. "How can you say that? You knew her. You cared about her."

Light danced along the strong lines of his jaw. His blue eyes were somber and almost navy in the darkness.

"Because it's my job," Anthony said, "and by the sounds of things it's your job too. We can't find out what happened to someone if we're not willing to ask the hard questions that the people who love her don't want to even consider. For example, why would she leave a bar with someone she had only just met? Did he offer her something she wanted? Like drugs? Was she engaging in risky behavior? Was she trying to escape one of the people she was there with? Predators are very skilled at knowing how to lure their prey into an isolated place. If Cassidy was lured from the bar that night, what was she lured with?"

Like Tessa had been lured to the island with

the promise of finding out what had happened to Cassidy.

She turned back and kept walking. He was right. They did need to answer those questions. But somehow it felt like a betrayal to even ask them. Like they were siding with the people who'd shamed Cassidy, speculated about her lifestyle and called her "troubled" on television.

The ground sloped upward, and it was clear that they were climbing uphill. The light in Anthony's hand was definitely getting fainter by the minute. It wouldn't be long until it went out altogether. The sound of the rain grew louder around them. The air grew lighter ahead of them. They were approaching an exit.

"Does knowing her body was found at the cottage cast anything we already know in a new light?" Anthony asked.

"I don't know," she said, thankful he'd changed the subject. "Later that night, two teenagers were spotted trying to hitchhike on the highway. A boy and a girl who seemed about Cassidy's age. Maybe she and whoever she was with were trying to make their way back to the cottage. But that doesn't explain how her cell phone and wallet were traveling south—"

A sudden and deafening crack shook the air. The air went dark. She could hear rocks falling. Something was roaring toward them. Then she felt the rush of earth and water plow into her body, knocking her back off her feet. She hit the ground. She tried to scream but dirty water cascaded over her, filling her lungs and forcing her down. The ground ahead of them had caved in, sending the once dormant river rushing toward them, threatening to drown them.

In an instant, Tessa vanished underneath the water.

"Tessa!" He shouted her name over the din of the roaring river.

Help me, Lord! I have to find her! She has to be okay!

The water surged past his knees. It was dark brown and thick with dirt and branches.

"Anthony!" Her voice echoed through the tunnel. It was faint but strong. Relief filled his core.

"Hang on!" he called. "I'm coming!"

He dropped the light in his breast pocket and ran back down the tunnel. Water beat against the back of his legs, threatening to knock him down. Then he saw her, clinging to the side of the tunnel ahead of him, and realized she'd been dragged the length of the average supermarket before managing to find her footing again. He reached for her hand. She stumbled into his chest. He braced his legs and wrapped both arms around her.

"Are you okay?" he asked.

"Yeah," she said. "The tunnel must've caved in ahead of us."

And now a mass of water and debris was coming their way, growing heavier and higher by the moment. If they didn't get out of the tunnels soon they'd both be buried alive.

"Come on," he said. He grabbed her hand, and they jogged back through the water toward the narrow shaft of light that cut through the ceiling ahead. They reached the sinkhole. He looked up. The rain had petered off to a light drizzle again, but the stone walls ran slick with water. "You go first. I'll give you a boost up."

He let go of her hand, then linked his fingers in front of him to create a step. She planted her right foot into his hands, put one hand on his shoulder and started climbing. But she'd only managed to climb up a couple of feet before he heard her cry out in frustration and watched as she lost her footing and tumbled toward him again. He caught her in his arms and set her back down. The water was almost up to her waist.

"Let me know when you're ready to try again," he said.

"I can't," she said. "It's too slippery. I can't get a grip."

Anthony reached up and pressed both hands against opposite sides of the shaft. The rock was rough beneath his palms.

"It won't be pretty," he said, "but my wingspan is wide enough, that if I brace my hands and my feet against opposite walls, like an X, I should be able to climb straight up like a spider in a drainpipe." Then he looked back at her. Her eyes were dark and luminous in her face. Wet curls traced delicate lines down her cheeks. Gently he lifted a long strand of hair and tucked it behind her ear. His fingers lingered on her skin. "But what about you? I don't wanna leave you alone down here."

"I'll be fine," she said. She didn't step away from his touch. Instead, she reached up and linked her fingers through his. "You get up there, lower something down for me and then I'll climb up after you. Easy-peasy. Nothing to worry about. Just go."

His breath tightened in his chest. She was

right, and yet somehow there was something inside him that didn't want to leave her.

She stepped toward him and slid her arms around his neck. His hands wrapped around her waist, and he pulled her in for the kind of deep and enveloping hug that something inside him had been longing to give her for years. He felt the furtive brush of her lips on his cheek. Then just as quickly as they embraced they let go.

"You told me you have a really good vertical jump," she said. "Now go."

Actually, he'd told her it was excellent.

He pulled the light from his pocket and pressed it into her hand. Then he leaped, feeling every atom of skill he'd developed on the basketball court surging through his legs. He flung his arms and legs out and caught himself by bracing his hands and feet against the wall on either side. He slid a few inches back down, then stopped as his grip held. He let out a long breath and started to climb. He could hear the sound of the water rushing beneath him along with Tessa's encouraging words calling up. And he remembered how he'd always felt stronger and more capable with her cheering him on. His limbs strained and ached like they were on fire. His hands scraped against the rock, and his knees bruised against the wall. He gritted his teeth, resisted the urge to look down and kept climbing.

The sky above him grew closer. Then he reached the top. He slid one hand over the edge and grabbed ahold of what he thought was a solid rock, but it broke loose under his grasp, nearly sending him tumbling back down the shaft again. He jammed his feet into the walls as hard as he could and pressed himself up again, this time waiting until he could actually get his head up through the hole and look around before trying again.

The forest lay dense and empty. Faint rain pattered against the leaves. He pushed both elbows into the mud, hauled himself up over the ledge and looked down.

Darkness fell beneath him. The last faint vestiges of the flashlight were finally gone.

"Tessa!" he called. "Where are you?"

"I'm here!" her voice echoed back to him. "I just got knocked down, and the light went out. The water's up to my chest, and I've got pretty big branches coming down at me now."

Help me, Lord, I need to get her out of there and fast.

He looked around for anything that he could use as a rope to pull her up and came up empty.

So he yanked off his jacket, tied one sleeve around his fist, lay down on his stomach and lowered the other end down.

"Here, grab this," he called, "and I'll haul you up."

"I see it," she responded, "sort of."

He could hear the sound of her body sloshing in the water below him as she jumped for it. Then he felt a tug on his wrist as her weight fell into his arm. But no sooner did he feel the strain of her starting to climb than his jacket went slack again, and he heard her cry out in frustration.

"Are you okay?"

"It's not long enough," she replied. "I have to jump up to get a grip on it and even then it's only my fingertips. The water's flowing faster and I'm having a hard time getting a foothold."

He wasn't wearing a belt. His shirt wouldn't provide much more length. He didn't want to risk taking off his boots. Then it hit him—he yanked off his bulletproof vest.

"Okay," he shouted. "I've found a solution." He fastened his jacket sleeve around the vest and tied it tight. "Just grab on. Don't argue with me, okay? We don't have time for a fight right now."

This time he tied the cuff of his jacket to his

wrist before wrapping it around his forearm once for good measure to compensate for the extra weight the vest would add. He dropped it down. There was a moment of silence.

Then she called, "Got it."

He felt her weight fall into his arm again. But this time he could tell she was solid. He leaned back and pulled. A moment later he'd hoisted her up high enough that she could plant her feet. Then he could feel her climbing up, step by step. Moments later he saw her. She'd stuck both of her arms through the bulletproof vest, using it to support her torso as she walked up the shaft. Then her head rose through the hole. He reached for her, grabbed her by both forearms and pulled her out. She collapsed on the ground beside him, panting.

"Thank you," she said.

"No problem."

She took a deep breath and stood. So did he. Something rustled in the trees. Then a large man in a bright yellow RCMP weatherproof jacket and navy RCMP cap stepped into the clearing and raised what looked like a police-issue Smith & Wesson.

"Get down on the ground," he shouted. "Hands where I can see them."

SIX

Instinctively Anthony's hand went for the lanyard where he carried his badge before realizing the masked men had taken it when they'd relieved him of his gun, wallet and phone.

"I'm Sergeant Anthony Jones," he identified himself loudly, "RCMP Major Crimes Unit." He remained standing and raised both hands out in front of his chest at shoulder height and spread his fingers to show that his hands were empty.

The other RCMP officer hesitated, like he'd stepped onto an unfamiliar stage and momentarily forgotten his lines. He was a large man with an even larger fluorescent windbreaker, in his late twenties, with a dark scar running down the side of his thin nose and faint curls in his short red hair. Then he holstered his weapon and reached inside his jacket to pull out an RCMP badge on a lanyard.

"Constable Wilson Newman," he said. "Zablocie sent me to get you off this island."

Relief rolled off Anthony's shoulders.

"Very nice to meet you," Anthony said. He strode forward and stuck out his hand. Wilson met him halfway, and the men shook hands. "Zablocie said he might be reaching out to you. I'm sure glad to see that he did."

"Sorry for all the drama," Wilson said, "but you guys are so wet and muddy I wasn't sure who I was stumbling on." He ran his hands down his baggy jeans, then glanced past Anthony to where Tessa stood one step behind him. "You must be Tessa Watson."

He stretched out his hand toward her, but instead of shaking it she just crossed her arms and nodded. Huh. Was she worried that Wilson was going to handcuff and arrest her if she stuck her hands out? Anthony wondered. After all, he had shown up with his weapon drawn and ordered them down on the ground.

"Come on," Wilson said with a good-natured chuckle and wave of his hand. "Let's get you out of here. I've got a boat moored not far from here."

"You didn't run into any trouble getting here?" Anthony asked. "Or see anyone?"

Wilson shook his head. His eyebrow rose.

"No," he said. "I did see two motorboats leaving the island as I was arriving. Is there something going on?"

"We ran into three armed men," Anthony said. "All three were masked, with sunglasses and hats. They tried to abduct Miss Watson, but I intercepted them. We don't know where they are now—although one of them stole my boat. We can't discount the possibility that one of them is still on the island."

"All the more reason we should hurry," Wilson said. He turned as if to lead them. "This way."

"Wait!" Tessa said and Anthony realized it was the first time he'd heard her say anything since Wilson had stepped out of the trees. "I left a backpack and some of my belongings in a clearing. We need to go there first."

"All right," Wilson said with an amiable grin. "Point the way."

Tessa gestured to the southwest, and they started walking single file through the forest and over the rocks up toward the center of the island. They walked slowly and carefully, keeping their eyes and ears open for any Anthony had expected Tessa to lead the way. But instead, she held back and let Wilson lead, as if she wanted to keep her eyes on

Wilson and didn't want him behind her. After a while Anthony noticed that Tessa's footsteps were lagging, as if her legs were so tired from their ordeal that she was struggling to find the energy to move. Before long she was a good dozen paces behind Wilson. Anthony fell back to join her. His hand brushed her elbow.

"Is everything okay?" Anthony asked, softly. She shook her head. "What's wrong?"

But instead of answering his questions, she took his hand and tugged it to get him to slow down their pace even more.

She leaned toward Anthony. "I don't trust him," she said.

Yeah, he could tell that much.

"I'm not going to let him arrest you—"

"Because you're planning to do it yourself?" she finished.

He pressed his lips together. They still hadn't unlinked their hands, and he could feel her fingers in his.

"He reminds me of someone," she added. "But I don't know who."

"Do you think he's connected to Cassidy's case somehow?"

"I don't know."

"Neither do I," Anthony said. "But Zablocie trusts him. The longer we stay on the island, the greater the risk that those masked men are going to reappear around the next rock. So, we let Wilson get us safely off the island, and then we make a plan from there. What are we going back to the camp for, specifically? I thought the only things you had left there were supplies, things like duct tape and a tarp. Are you sure, whatever it is, it's worth further risking our lives on?"

"Nothing we need specifically," she said. "I'm just trying to buy myself some time to think, before we blindly hop in his boat and let him take us wherever he's decided we should go."

Anthony blinked. "What?"

Was she serious with this? Was she actually trying to waste time in a dangerous place that could get them killed?

Wilson glanced back. Both of his eyebrows rose this time. Quickly, Anthony pulled his fingers from Tessa's. Heat rose to the back of his neck when he realized Wilson had seen them holding hands. The last thing he needed was for someone in law enforcement to think he was having an unprofessional relationship with Tessa. Let alone pass that impression back to Zablocie.

He had to keep this relationship professional.

Despite the way he'd held her in his arms back in the tunnels, how she'd brushed a kiss across his cheeks or the fact their hands kept somehow finding each other's. Anthony was still a cop. Tessa was still a suspect. And he'd do well to remember that.

They kept walking. Anthony waited until he was sure that Wilson was out of earshot again.

"Look, I was pretty understanding about the fact you blew off my colleagues this morning," he said. "I genuinely tried to see things from your point of view. But this is different, because right now we are quite literally stuck on an island." He fought to keep his voice from rising. "We have no boat, no phone, no weapons to defend ourselves with, no way off this island and no way to contact the outside world. Not that long ago I was stuck in a tunnel thinking about how I'd build a makeshift raft out of an air mattress."

Anthony sighed. He didn't need her to trust Wilson. But he did need her to trust him. And after everything they'd been through, what could Anthony possibly do to prove to her that he was worthy of her trust? He remembered that Tessa had told him she'd thought she'd been stalked for years, and after everything that had happened today it was clear that she had good reason to be suspicious. But he also remembered that she hadn't talked to her parents in years, despite how close they'd once been.

"What happened to you, Tessa?" he asked. "When did you become so suspicious of everyone? What can I do to get you to trust me?"

She didn't look at him and just kept walking forward.

"You're a really great guy," she said. "But you don't get it."

"You're absolutely right I don't," Anthony said. "Because you won't explain it to me."

Once again, she didn't answer.

His eyes scanned the gray skies above.

Help me, Lord. I am frustrated beyond words. I don't even know what to pray right now. You know better than anyone just how much I cared about Tessa, and nothing she's thinking makes any sense to me. All I know is that I feel lost and stuck, and I need Your help.

Then a thought crossed his mind. He ran forward and caught up with Wilson.

"Do you have your phone handy?" Anthony asked. "I just realized that neither of us has called Chief Superintendent Zablocie and given him an update. Mind if I give him a quick shout and fill him in?"

"Good idea," Wilson said. He stopped walking, and so did Anthony. Wilson reached into his jacket pocket and pulled out his cell phone without batting an eyelash. "We should keep the chief superintendent in the loop."

He held the phone between them and opened up the screen that showed his recent calls. Anthony immediately recognized the top number as Zablocie's. Wilson had received three calls from him over the course of the morning. The last one had been less than half an hour ago. Wilson pushed the button to call Zablocie.

"Here you go," Wilson said.

He handed it to Anthony while it rang. Anthony looked down at the screen. It was almost a quarter to two. He had barely two hours left before the deadline his boss had given him, and they were still on an island.

"Hello!" The chief superintendent's unmistakable voice boomed down the phone line. "Constable Newman. What's going on? Have you had any success in tracking down Sergeant Jones and Miss Watson?"

"Hey, boss," he said. "It's me. Anthony. I'm here with Constable Newman and Tessa Watson."

He heard Zablocie let out what sounded like a sigh of relief.

"Glad to hear it," Zablocie said.

Anthony looked over at Tessa. She'd stopped just a few feet away, just out of arm's reach. Silent questions filled her eyes.

"How's Cinderella?" Anthony asked, remembering what Violet had told him about the goldfish that Zablocie's granddaughter had given him.

"You mean Rapunzel?" his boss said dryly. "Still swimming in circles. You're welcome to drop by and give her some fish flakes once you've wrapped up the case."

"How did you know where we were?" Anthony asked.

"Your sister called my office when you didn't check in with her," his boss said. "She told me that Tessa had escaped by kayak, and you'd followed her in a rented motorboat, and she provided us with aerial maps of the surrounding islands. I passed all this on to Constable Newman and asked him to search for you."

Anthony had located the right island by spotting the tip of Tessa's kayak sticking out from behind a rock and the telltale signs that someone had recently been on the beach. He expected Wilson had found them in a similar way.

"We've had some trouble," Anthony said.

He quickly filled his boss in on an abbreviated version of what happened with the three masked men on the island. He ended with the fact Wilson had seen two boats leave the island, which he guessed were the masked men's boat and the one he'd brought. His boss whistled under his breath.

"Well, all the better that you're bringing Miss Watson in," Zablocie said. "How long will it take for you to get her in to a station?"

"My truck's in Princess," Anthony said, evading the specifics of the question. "It's about a two-hour drive to Whistler or a little over three to Vancouver. But first we need to get off the island. I'll call you from my truck with an update."

Hopefully with Tessa by his side in the passenger seat, having agreed to come in for questioning. Anthony wasn't quite sure what he'd do if she didn't.

"For now just focus on getting Miss Watson to Whistler for questioning," Zablocie said. "Once she's been processed and interrogated there, I'll arrange to have her transported to Vancouver. Right now I've got a grieving family on my hands demanding answers."

"Understood," Anthony said, then added,

"but with all due respect I think it's short-sighted to focus the investigative efforts on Tessa. I believe someone is framing her as a diversion to keep us from figuring out what actually happened. There's been a credible threat against Tessa's life."

"And that threat is all the more reason to bring her in immediately," Zablocie said. "The sooner we question her, the sooner we can rule her out as a suspect, if she did indeed have nothing to do with the crime. Not to mention it'll be a lot harder for whoever is after her to threaten her life when she's safely behind bars instead of running around the woods. We can't discount the possibility that whoever is after her is a current or former accomplice, or someone she's crossed during the commission of a crime. Either way, the fact someone's out to get her is hardly exonerating."

Anthony looked at Tessa. Her beautiful hazel eyes were locked on his face. And along with the strength and determination he'd grown used to seeing, another emotion flickered there—hope. His chest ached as if his heart was being pulled in two different directions at once. He broke her gaze.

Please, Lord, don't make me choose between protecting Tessa and doing my job.

"So you'll bring her in?" Zablocie asked. His voice was as firm and unflinching as steel.

"I will," Anthony said.

Even if he had to handcuff Tessa to do it. And even though he knew that if he did, she'd never forgive him.

He ended the call and handed the phone back to Wilson.

"Everything okay?" Tessa asked.

"Yup," he said without meeting her eye. "All good with Zablocie. Come on. The sooner we get off this island the better."

They started walking again. This time he stayed closer to Wilson to discourage Tessa from trying to strike up a private conversation. He'd confirmed Zablocie had sent Wilson—which hadn't really been in doubt in his mind, but should hopefully show Tessa that he had taken her concerns seriously enough to verify their rescuer. He could feel Tessa at his elbow, and he knew she was trying to get his attention. But the conversation with his boss weighed heavy on his mind. If only there was some option other than taking her in against her will, but he couldn't exactly let her run either.

They reached the top of a hill. The rain had now ended completely, but the air smelled damp, and the gray sky hung heavy above them. Tessa pointed to the left, and Anthony could see the remains of her campsite about a fifteen-minute walk away on a higher outcropping of rock.

"My boat's straight ahead down that slope," Wilson said. He pointed down and slightly to the right where a glimmer of gray-blue water peeked through the branches. "It's a pretty steep climb."

Tessa's camp and Wilson's boat were in almost opposite directions. The trees rustled to their right. They weren't alone on the island. Someone was there and coming closer.

Instinctively, he reached out a protective arm, wrapped it around Tessa's shoulders and then pulled them both behind the relative protection of a large outcrop of rock. Wilson joined them.

The sound of footsteps and breaking branches grew closer.

"You saw two boats leaving the island," Anthony said.

"I did," Wilson said. "Maybe they came back."

The trees parted. The man in the white mask and mirrored sunglasses burst through the bushes. He aimed his gun at them and fired in their direction. The bullet ricocheted off the rocks. Wilson crouched up and returned fire.

Anthony grabbed Tessa's hand and shouted, "Run!"

She felt Anthony pull her up to her feet, then he dropped her hand and they started running, heading in the direction where Wilson had indicated his boat was anchored. He'd said the ground was steep. That was an understatement. The ground seemed to spill down in a mass of brush, twisting roots and rocks in front of her. It forced her to weave back and forth down the slope, so that she ran to the right for twenty or thirty steps, then turned around and ran back the other direction, in a much longer zigzag path. She could hear Anthony a few steps behind her, and beyond him, somewhere in the forest she could hear Wilson exchanging gunfire with one of the masked men who'd tried to kidnap her.

It hit her that, for the first time since this whole ordeal had started this morning, Tessa was running blind, without a mental map of where she was going or a plan of what she'd do when she got there. Desperately her eyes tried to scan for Wilson's boat in the trees, but she could barely even see the water, let alone the shoreline.

Her feet tumbled faster and faster until she was practically tripping over her steps as she zigged and zagged down the slope. She looked forward, planning her path just a few moments at a time. A giant boulder loomed ahead of her feet. From there, she'd have to stop abruptly, leap straight down a couple of feet and then run back to the left again.

The trees moved. Before she could even think, let alone react, the skinny man in the mustard-colored hat, dark sunglasses and yellow animal mask stepped out in front of her, almost as if he'd been lying in wait. He startled. There was a rifle on a thick strap across his body, and he fumbled for the trigger as he tried to aim it at her.

Time froze. Instinctively, she crouched low, as if somehow she could shrink herself.

"Stay down!" Anthony shouted from behind her.

Then Anthony leaped. He vaulted over her and launched himself at the man in the yellow mask. For a split second she thought he was about to tackle him. Instead, she watched Anthony let a fist fly across the man's jaw before his own feet had even hit the ground. The blow knocked the man back against the ground and caused him to drop the weapon.

Anthony landed on the balls of his feet and lunged for him, like he was instinctively reaching to grab the rifle and disarm him before the man's brain caught up with the fact he was wearing it on a strap around his neck. Instead, Anthony reached for the man's face, knocked off his hat, yanked off his sunglasses and tried to pull down the man's gaiter mask. The mask only came down an inch, but it was enough for Tessa to see the man's partial face. His hair was buzz-cut bald. His eyes were gray, bloodshot and sunken. What's more, she was sure that she'd seen this face somewhere before.

A name swam to the front of her mind: Lewis.

Lewis Fowler works at his uncle's car dealership and has been in trouble with the police a few times, mostly for drug stuff, fighting and theft... He was eighteen when Cassidy disappeared...

But she didn't have a strong enough memory of what Lewis's face had actually looked like to know for sure if she was right.

Anthony stood over him. "Who are you?" he demanded. "What do you want with Tessa?"

Before the man could answer, she heard the

sound of vile threats bellowing from some-where in the trees behind them and realized it had been a few moments since she'd heard the bangs of gunfire. Now it sounded like the man in the green mask had joined his white-masked counterpart. They were both shout-ing and threatening to kill Wilson, while the constable loudly identified himself as an of-ficer of the law.

She watched as Anthony hesitated, torn between the man at his feet, the fellow offi-cer now fighting for his life and his need to get Tessa to safety. A bullet whizzed through the branches and struck a tree a few inches to their right, shattering the bark. She felt splin-ters strike her body. The yellow-masked man took advantage of the distraction and slithered backward through the woods. She willed her mind to remember his face.

"Tessa, run!" Anthony said. "I'm going back to help Wilson."

"I'm not leaving you," she said.

Neither of them would be safer alone than they'd be together.

Then she heard but couldn't see Wilson crashing through the forest above them.

"Go!" Wilson shouted. "I'll meet you at the boat!"

Run for the boat, chase after the man in the yellow mask or go back for Wilson—there was no right answer, only the one most likely to get them out of there alive.

Gunfire rang out above them again. She still couldn't see Wilson but guessed the chaos erupting above them meant that he was being chased. She kept running down the slope toward the water, and relief poured over her core as she felt Anthony running just one step behind her. Tessa had no idea what she'd have done if Anthony hadn't come with her. Would she have kept going or gone after him?

Their footsteps reached the shore. It was rocky and uneven, with huge stones that jutted out into the water. They ran along the water's edge and a few steps later, she could finally see the boat. It was on their right and tied precariously to a tree that grew sideways out of the end of a slab of rock, cutting through the water like a sharp and uneven dock. They ran for it.

She prayed, as thoughts tumbled through her mind, asking God to help them reach the boat safely, to help her, Anthony and Wilson get off the island, and to help her remember the fleeting glimpse of the face she saw without enough clarity to confirm it was in fact Cassidy's former colleague Lewis.

Leaves and rocks tumbled down the hill slightly ahead and on their left. It was Wilson. He was scrambling straight down the hill toward the water, taking a much steeper, more dangerous and direct way down the hill to the boat than they had. A deep red gash cut into Wilson's left sleeve and blood smeared on the bright yellow jacket.

"Are you okay?" Anthony asked. Concern filled his voice. "You're bleeding."

Wilson chuckled through gritted teeth.

"Yeah," Wilson said. "No biggie. This big guy caught me with the tip of his knife. But I got a decent blow in, and he fell back." Something almost like pride tinged his voice. "If it hadn't been a rescue operation, I'd have slapped cuffs on him, but he turned tail and evaded capture. You guys go ahead, I'll cover you."

Anthony shook his head.

"You're injured," he said. "You get yourself safely in the boat, and we'll all get out of here."

Tessa crossed the rock first. Gingerly, she made her way across the slippery and uneven ground, using the horizontal tree to maintain her balance. The motorboat was small, with white seats and silver sides that seemed to gleam in the gloom. It floated a good six feet away. She grabbed the rope and pulled it closer, internally wincing as she heard it scrape across the rock. Anthony reached her side. He leaned past her and steadied the boat while she scrambled over the side.

"Now you go," he told Wilson. "As the one with the longest legs, it falls on me to untie the rope. You can cover us from the bow while Tessa and I get us untied and push off."

He looked ready to argue. There was an odd bravado about the younger officer, Tessa noted, like he was trying to prove himself. She wondered if he was intimidated by Anthony. Wilson climbed across the rocks, tumbled into the boat and stumbled to the front. It shook under his weight. Anthony was now the only one left on shore.

"Do you have a first aid kit?" Tessa asked. "We need to get your arm patched up."

Wilson shook his head. "It's fine. Seriously. It looks much worse than it is."

Wilson stood at the wheel, pulled his weapon and aimed defensively toward the rocky hillside. Silence had fallen from the island now. Her eyes scanned the rocks and trees for their unseen attackers, but she couldn't see or hear any glimpse of them. There was something wrong about the behavior of their masked pursuers. They'd left the island but then they'd returned? They'd fired guns into the trees, and then one of them had stabbed Wilson? And now they'd suddenly disappeared again. Where had they gone? Were they reloading, regrouping or making their way down the hill toward them?

Anthony untied the boat and tossed Tessa the rope. She caught it and then stretched out her hand toward Anthony. The very end of his fingertips gripped hers. Then Anthony leaped into the boat while she pulled him in to her.

"All good," Anthony called. "Let's get out of here."

Wilson holstered his weapon, then yanked a bandana from his back pocket and tied it around the cut. He started the boat. It flew backward so quickly it rocked, then Wilson spun the boat around, and they sped away from the island. A final and unexpected spray of bullets struck the water, but they were already out of range.

Tessa climbed out of her seat, took Anthony's hand and led him to the long bench seat in the back of the boat. She collapsed onto it, and he sat beside her. For a long moment they sat there, side by side, with their fingers still linked. Then he pulled away and looked behind them. So did she.

"I don't see them," he said. "But this boat is fast enough they won't be able to catch us before we get back to Princess." Then he leaned closer to her, and his voice dropped. "Are you okay?"

"You ask me that an awful lot," she said.

His eyebrow rose. "Does that bother you?"

"No, it's kind of comforting."

She smiled weakly and Anthony did too.

"I don't know if I'm right about this," she said. "But I think the man you partially unmasked is Lewis Fowler, one of the people Cassidy was with the night she disappeared."

Anthony's blue eyes widened. He leaned back.

"Are you sure?"

"No," she said. "But I have a lot of photos of him, both then and now, in my computer database that we can compare our memories to. My laptop is back at the hotel. Hopefully when I load up the pics, you and I should know pretty quickly if I'm right."

Anthony ran his hand over the back of his neck. She imagined he was planning to take her straight to Whistler or wherever for questioning. Stopping by her hotel room to pore over her files of Cassidy's disappearance hadn't been part of the equation. It had been a couple of hours since she and Anthony had struck an uneasy truce. They'd never discussed what would happen to that truce once they reached the shore.

"I still don't trust Wilson," she admitted. "Even though your boss sent him and obviously trusts him, there's just something about him that sets my teeth the wrong way. It's like he's trying too hard."

To her surprise Anthony nodded. "I know what you mean. Most officers learn pretty early on that this career isn't a good fit for wannabe heroes. Sure, there are moments of valor, but it's more important to get everyone out alive."

He frowned and she was wondering if he was thinking of his childhood hero, General Alberto McClean, who'd calmly talked a gunman into surrendering on live television.

"I should get his phone and call Zablocie," Anthony said.

He started to get up, but she grabbed his hand and squeezed his fingers.

"Wait," she said. He sat back down. She closed her eyes and prayed for wisdom. When she opened her eyes again, Anthony's gaze was intent on her face. "I have all these files on Cassidy's case. I want to get to my database and go through the files and verify if we really saw who I thought I did. I also want to refresh myself before I'm interviewed. I won't have access to them once I go in for custody. If they decide to hold me it could be a while before I can access anything on my computer, and I'm convinced there's information on there that will help us solve what's happened to her."

"You know we'll just get a subpoena for all your devices," Anthony said, almost regretfully.

"With all due respect, it'll take a very long time for someone to pore through it all," she said, "and there's a risk stuff will fall through the cracks."

Anthony's mouth opened but she held up a hand before he could answer. She pulled her other hand from his.

"But I know your boss only gave you a few hours to bring me in for questioning," she went on, quickly. "You, he and the RCMP are under a lot of pressure to solve this case. He's got Cassidy's grieving family to answer to, and he can't just let me go. You know how important it is that we find Cassidy's killer."

"I do," he said.

"And that's why it's in my best interest that I don't end up in jail and let the cops pin it on someone who didn't do it. So, what if we find another way? A compromise. Instead of just sticking me in the back of the car and driving me two hours to an RCMP division before anyone starts questioning me, why don't we do it back at the inn? I have a suite."

At this, his eyebrows rose.

"Police do interview suspects on location without bringing them in all the time," she went on. "You can interview me on camera, record it and live stream it for whoever else is working on this. You've only got two hours, give or take, before Zablocie's press conference. Why not make the most of that time and speed things up? It will save a lot of time. You can start the interview right away and get the RCMP the right leads a lot faster, and they can then start pursuing them. Zablocie can go into his media briefing with actual solid information instead of some wild theory that I'm somehow the killer. It will help them solve the case faster. You know it's a smart move and best for the investigation."

And best for her too.

She turned away from his gaze, looked to the shoreline and prayed. Anthony was quiet for a long moment, and she suspected he was praying too.

"You're right," he said, finally. "It's a good idea and best for the investigation. I think I can talk Zablocie into it. We can use my laptop. It's in my truck."

A long sigh of relief left her lungs.

Thank You, God.

"If we do this," he said, "do you promise you won't run?"

"Do you promise you won't arrest me?" she asked.

He didn't answer. Neither did she.

SEVEN

Less than half an hour later, Tessa found herself back at the inn, pacing in front of her laptop as it sat open on the bed. Faces scrolled in front of her in a veritable rogue's gallery of people who were connected to Cassidy's disappearance. There were 156 images, some of which were of the same person at various ages.

The first thing she and Anthony had done when they'd gotten back to her suite was fire up her database and pull up pictures of Lewis Fowler. The most recent photo she had of him was a mug shot from a minor arrest two years ago, and both she and Anthony agreed immediately that was the man in the yellow mask. Not that police wouldn't still need proof to charge him. Anthony said he'd make sure the man was brought in for questioning, which wouldn't be too hard since, as a probation condition, he wasn't supposed to be outside Ontario, let alone trying to kidnap a woman on the other side of the country.

Did that mean the other two men on the island had been linked to the colleagues Cassidy had been with the night she disappeared?

Wilson had gone into the bathroom that adjoined the living room in order to clean up the cut on his arm, assuring them both yet again that it was minor and he didn't need help. Then Anthony had told Tessa he was going to call Chief Superintendent Zablocie just as soon as he'd checked in with his sister, Violet, to let her know they were okay. And Tessa had gone into the bedroom to clean the mud off herself and change into some clean clothes. He'd gotten his laptop and a backup, pay-as-you-go cell phone from the truck.

Last she'd seen Wilson he'd finished up in the bathroom and then gone out on to the balcony, where he'd stood talking to someone on his own phone, purportedly to give Anthony some privacy while he talked to Zablocie in the suite's living room. She didn't think that the two cops had purposely spaced themselves out, with each of them blocking one of the suite's two exits to keep her from trying to make a hasty escape. But that was the result.

Any moment now Anthony would knock on

the door and tell her that his laptop was all set up and Zablocie was ready to go.

Tessa wasn't ready to be interviewed. Not yet. Not until she knew exactly how she was going to clear her name and figure out who'd killed Cassidy and framed her. There had to be something in her copious files that would explain everything, get her off the hook and send the police flying straight to the location of the real killer, or killers, to cart them away in handcuffs.

There'd been three masked men on the island. If, as they believed, the man in the yellow mask was Lewis, could she figure out the identity of the other two? Katie Masters was ruled out because she was barely five feet tall, although she did have a husband, brother and friends. Tom Groff or Cole Rook both had the height to be the man in the white mask, but she had no idea if either had a wrist tattoo or why either would go from catering and lawyering respectively into kidnapping. Drew Roberts matched the man in the green mask's height. But that was all. He didn't have the bulbous nose or the straight dark hair. He was a redhead like Wilson. True, rumor was he'd had plastic surgery back when he'd been trying to make it as an actor. Plus he'd been really skinny back then; the most recent picture she had of him was when he was a teenager.

If anything, Lewis had been an obvious one. He was the only one with a criminal history, and his record was twice as long as Tessa's arm for a string of unbelievably petty crimes, like filling up at the gas station and driving off without paying and trying to return stolen merchandise. As far as she could tell, the only things that kept Lewis out of doing any serious jail time were the fact he had a legitimate job at his family's car dealership and someone kept paying for his bail and lawyers. Plus the fact he'd been arrested several times and had an array of different mug shots meant they had something recent to compare to.

But now Tessa had a lead. A major lead. One they didn't have before. Something even more solid and tangible than the bracelet still sitting in the hotel room safe. It had to mean something.

She glanced through the door's peephole at Anthony. He was still on the phone, and his back was to her. The door was surprisingly soundproof. But somehow she could tell from his posture that he'd wrapped up the call to his sister and was now on the phone with his boss. His shoulders were straighter, he was standing taller and while she couldn't hear his words, something about the way his hand cut through the air, punctuating his side of the conversation, made her think that while Zablocie was a tough sell, Anthony was convincing him.

She stepped away from the door and sat on the side of the bed. In a weird way, she missed Anthony. Even though he was only a few feet away and they were about to spend the next couple of hours, or even longer, talking on camera. But for a brief moment in time, back on the island, Anthony had been her ally—her partner even. He'd been by her side, he'd listened to her and, while they'd argued, they'd also had each other's backs. For the first time in longer than she could remember she hadn't felt completely alone.

Now he was a cop and she was a suspect again.

A swell of emotions that she didn't quite know how to put into words tightened her chest, pressing against her lungs until she struggled to breathe. This aching feeling in her core, whatever it was, had been there every day since Cassidy had vanished, and nothing she did— no matter how hard she worked or how many cases she solved—had managed to ever quell it.

She slipped from the bed, knelt beside it and

closed her eyes. She couldn't remember the last time she'd actually knelt to pray, but she was pretty sure it had been back when she was younger, and her parents had still been enforcing kneeling to pray at bedtime.

She tried to find the words to ask God for help. But the truth was, she didn't think she deserved it. If she'd handled everything better the night she'd snuck out to rescue Cassidy from Kevin's party, maybe her parents wouldn't have banned her from taking a camp job that summer. Then maybe Tessa would've been there at the cottage the weekend she disappeared. Maybe Tessa would've been able to stop her from leaving the bar with some unidentified stranger, and from getting back together with Kevin, or from dating somebody else just like him. If only she'd told Cassidy that she loved her no matter what, instead of sending her an angry letter...

God, if I'd just tried harder, been kinder, been more understanding, found the right words to say... If only I'd been a better person, then Cassidy might still be alive.

The weight on her heart was growing heavier.

God? My mom told me that whenever I feel bad inside that's because You are angry or dis-

appointed with me. But I don't think Anthony believes that. Because Anthony has never talked about You that way or prayed like he believes that's true about You.

She curled her knees into her chest, folded her arms on top of them and rested her chin on top of her arms.

All I know is there's this weight in my heart that I feel like I've been living with ever since the day Cassidy disappeared. I don't even know if it's a bad thing, because whatever it is, it's pushed me to solve crimes, protect people and even save lives. And I'm thankful for that. But sometimes it feels like it's suffocating me too. Lord, I don't even know what I'm praying for. I just know something's wrong, and I want to do my part to fix it.

There was a rap on the door. She raised her head and opened her eyes.

"Tessa?" Anthony called.

"Yeah? I'm here."

"Zablocie's given us the green light," Anthony said. "Needless to say he's not thrilled with the prospect of a remote interview. But he agrees that it's the most expedient option and will enable the RCMP to take action much faster to follow up on any potential leads. We're all in agreement that the most important thing right now is solving Cassidy's murder." He paused, and she wondered if he was weighing his words or waiting for her to answer. "As you suggested, it's going to be recorded. He'll also be watching the live stream, but we won't be able to see him. There may be other investigators watching the live feed, as well. Think of it as the technological version of a two-way mirror. I have to make sure you're one hundred percent aware that this will be an official police interview, on the record. You are under no obligation to talk to us without a lawyer present and anything you do or say can be used against you in subsequent legal action."

"Got it," she said. "Just give me a moment."

She ran her hands through her hair. She'd tried to wash the mud from the island off in the bathroom sink but could still feel knots under her fingers.

"Okay," Anthony said. "I'll be here. By the way, I got through to my sister. Violet says hi."

Silence fell on the other side of the door again. Tessa stood slowly and turned to face the mirror. She looked older and more tired than she remembered.

Help me, Lord. I can't do this on my own.

Then a thought crossed her mind. There was one person who knew about the case who she could trust. She sat down on the edge of her bed, turned her laptop around to face her and pulled up her contact book, hoping that Violet's cell phone number hadn't changed since they were teenagers. She plugged it into her video chat app and dialed.

"Hello?" Violet's face filled the screen. Tessa could tell by the angle that she'd answered the call on her cell phone, which she had propped up somewhere on her desk. Violet's indigo eyes were even more striking than Tessa had remembered and were framed beautifully with dusty blue eyeshadow and thick dark lashes. A pair of glasses sat perched on top of her braided hair. Her eyes widened and then she smiled. "Tessa! Hi! It's so good to see you!"

Tessa turned the volume down to keep from being overheard.

"It's good to see you too," Tessa said. "How are you?"

Violet laughed. "Surviving," she said. "Some bright spark forgot to cancel my office wedding-shower luncheon today, despite the fact my so-called fiancé called off the wedding a few weeks ago." She reached for the phone and turned the screen to show the pastel pink, blue and green cake that sat on a table at the side of the room. A few pieces were missing. "They also forgot to cancel the cake."

Tessa winced. "Yikes, I'm sorry," she said. "How is it?"

"Not good," Violet said, and set the phone back down on her desk so Tessa was looking at her face again. "But I'm eating it anyway."

Tessa laughed. This was definitely not what she'd expected to be talking about, and she debated thanking Violet for the reminder that there was a broader world outside the small room she was in, where thoughtless colleagues ordered garish cakes for canceled weddings.

"Look, I know it's more than a little unorthodox," Tessa said, "and I'm in no position to ask you a favor. I suspect all of the men who tried to kidnap me are either Cassidy's former colleagues, who were there the weekend she vanished, or somehow connected to them. But I'm going off old photos and I'm wondering if you can pull up anything more recent?"

"I can look," Violet said. "In my experience, some people look pretty much identical at twenty-eight to who they were at sixteen, while others are completely unrecognizable. Maybe somebody had prosthetics or wigs on underneath their masks." She started typing. "I thought you were going to ask me to look into Constable Wilson Newman's record. Anthony told me you think there's something off about him."

Tessa sat down. If she was honest, her unease about Wilson hadn't been the top thing on her mind. But now that Violet had brought it up she was definitely intrigued.

"I can't believe Anthony said that," Tessa admitted.

"I don't know why it would surprise you," Violet said. "He's one hundred percent convinced of your innocence. I know sometimes he talks like his is the only view of things that matters, but deep down I know he respects your opinion, a lot, and he cares about you. He wouldn't put his career on the line for just anybody."

Tessa opened her mouth, but no words came out.

"In Anthony's mind, he hasn't been in a relationship with anyone else since you two broke up," she added. "From my perspective, as his sister, he's tried going out for coffee or dinner with half a dozen people, but none ever made it past a second date. Because he can't stand being told that he's wrong about anything, but also gets bored with anyone who doesn't challenge him. Not that it's any of my business.

But he's my twin and I love him. Plus I'm all hopped up on rejection cake."

Violet turned to her computer and started typing.

"So, yes he told me that you didn't trust Wilson Newman and asked me to look into him," she went on. "But I'll tell you the same thing that I told him. He's got a pretty decent record. He was working in New Brunswick when Cassidy disappeared and has no link to her investigation. He's got a good solid history filled with plain old boring day-to-day police work. Nothing flashy or out of the ordinary."

Tessa pursed her lips and tried to square that with the memory of his bravado back on the island.

"Never married. No kids of his own. But he's close with his nieces and nephews, and coaches a kids' softball team. What didn't you like about him?"

"I don't know how to put it into words exactly," Tessa said. "Something about him just didn't feel right."

"I don't know what to tell you," Violet said.

She turned the phone around again so Tessa could see her computer screen. There was a picture of a large man in an RCMP police uniform with a short, cropped beard and amiable face, standing among a group of smiling kids.

And Tessa knew in an instant exactly what was wrong.

"That's not the man who rescued us," Tessa said. "Whoever that man is in the other room with Anthony right now, who showed up on that island in an RCMP jacket with Wilson Newman's badge and phone, he's an imposter."

"Good to see you," Chief Superintendent Zablocie said. "You're coming through nice and clear."

Anthony felt his spine straighten. "Good to see you too, sir."

Anthony's boss's face filled the screen of his laptop. Wade Zablocie had gray hair and the kind of square jaw that made his bushy 1980's style moustache look both distinguished and intimidating. He had no concrete idea how old the chief superintendent actually was, but rumor had it he was in his early seventies. Anthony could tell by the sound of shuffling feet that there were other people in his office, including the unseen tech guy who'd set up the call. But all he could see on his screen was his boss, and over his shoulder the beautiful black and orange goldfish now swimming in elegant circles.

"When is Tessa Watson joining us?" Zablocie asked.

Anthony shot a sideways glance to the door of the bedroom suite. It was still closed. What was taking Tessa so long?

"Soon," he said.

Anthony was about to knock on the door again when suddenly it swung open and there stood Tessa, in clean clothes, with a freshly washed face and a steely look in her eyes.

"Right. Shall we do this?" she asked.

Anthony blew out a breath in relief.

"And here she is," he said. "Tessa, meet my boss, Chief Superintendent of the Royal Canadian Mounted Police's Major Crimes Unit."

"Nice to meet you," Zablocie said. "Thank you for joining us today."

"You too," Tessa said. Her chin rose. "I look forward to clearing my name."

Zablocie nodded in response. She strode across the room toward the place where he'd set up his laptop on the coffee table, with two chairs sitting in front of the camera's field of vision. There was some activity on the screen, and then the picture switched to what Anthony's laptop's camera saw—just the two chairs and the door.

"Where's Wilson?" she asked.

"Outside on the balcony," Anthony said and gestured.

"Has your laptop started recording?" she asked. She leaned down before the laptop, and her face filled the screen. "Can your boss and potentially people at RCMP headquarters still see us right now?"

"They can," Anthony said.

"Does Wilson know we're being monitored live?" she asked. "Or that we've started recording?"

Her eyes fixed on where Wilson was standing, outside on the balcony. Wilson waved cheerfully.

"No and no." Anthony's forehead creased. "He wasn't there for any of the set-up conversation. Why?"

Before she could answer Wilson, opened the door and walked back in. He then leaned against the wall and crossed his arms. She smiled at Wilson politely.

Something was up with her. But what?

Tessa still hadn't really looked his way, let alone met his gaze. It was like a breaker switch had been tripped inside her. Her motions were focused and determined, like a woman on a mission. But missing was the telltale quiver she got in her bottom lip or the way her fists clenched at her side when she felt like she had to defend herself. Both of which he'd have expected to see, considering she was about to be interrogated about the murder of her best friend in front of an audience who might think she was guilty. But instead, her jaw was clenched and a thin smile crossed her lips that reminded him of an elastic band that was ready to snap.

Anthony walked over and laid a hand on Tessa's shoulder. The gesture was meant as supportive. But her muscles were so tight, she might as well have been carved out of stone. He stepped back.

"Are you okay?" Anthony asked, softly. "Do you want to talk about something before we start?"

She cut her eyes to the screen. "No, I'm good."

Anthony realized the moment he'd said the words how foolish they might've been. His boss was watching after all. This whole thing was being recorded. They were effectively standing in an interrogation room. Anthony could hardly be seen to be popping off for a quiet tête–à–tête. And yet, Tessa might be the smartest person he knew. If there was something she wanted him to know, surely she'd have somehow found some way to tell him.

Tessa sat down in one of the chairs in front of the laptop and a much smaller image of her appeared on the screen.

"Before we start," she said, "I'd love to do a quick review of everything. Maybe Corporal Wilson would be kind enough to help me chat things out and get my heads on straight."

She waved at the empty chair opposite her as if inviting Wilson to sit.

"He isn't part of the team working on this case," Anthony said.

Which she already knew. Anthony's phone rang in his pocket. He ignored it. It had to be Violet—nobody else had the number of his backup phone—and whatever she wanted to talk about could wait until after the interview.

"Well, actually," Wilson pushed off from the wall and took few steps toward her. "I have done quite a bit of reading up on this particular case."

"And as we all know, an outside perspective can sometimes be helpful," Tessa added.

Were the two of them kidding with this? Anthony cringed internally, knowing his boss and whoever else he'd brought on the tactical team was hearing this back-and-forth banter and realizing how unprofessional it sounded. She was a suspect in a murder investigation. Wilson was an officer from a completely different division. Anthony was the lead detective in charge, whose career was on the line, and it was like the two of them were reading lines from a script that Anthony hadn't been given a copy of.

"I would love to hear your theories on Cassidy Chase's disappearance," Tessa told Wilson with a smile so bright she might've been posing for a toothpaste commercial. "I've been building this giant research file on the case for years. Thousands and thousands of pictures and documents. Research on everybody connected to the case."

"Oh, really," Wilson said. He walked around to the side of the computer but stopped before he appeared on camera. "Where is it?"

"Online," she said. "I uploaded it to a private server so that I can access it from anywhere. I can even share it with the police during the interview, so that they can see everything I've collected on various people involved in the case."

Anthony's phone rang in his pocket again. This time he pulled it out, glanced at the screen and declined the call. Violet started calling back again immediately.

"You've been looped in to the fact that we

suspect one of the men who ambushed us on the island is Lewis Fowler, one of the five camp colleagues who were with Cassidy the day she disappeared?" Tessa asked.

"Mmm-hmm?" Wilson murmured noncommittally.

Anthony took a few steps back, to make sure he kept himself out of the frame and texted his sister.

Can't talk.
About to start interviewing Tessa.

Three dots appeared on the screen as Violet typed.

What's going on?
Is everything okay?!

He texted back.

We're fine.
Tessa's talking to Wilson right now on the video feed.

He slid the phone back in his pocket.

"I've been collecting dirt on Lewis for years and had a lot of recent mug shots to compare,"

Tessa went on. She leaned forward with her hands on her knees. "Now, if he was smart he'd have done what Drew Roberts did."

"And what did he do?" Wilson asked. His hand flinched toward what Anthony thought was his gun holster, but instead he grabbed his phone.

Two texts chimed and Anthony's phone started to ring again immediately. Whenever either Anthony or his sister sent a text they wanted the other to see right away they'd call and hang up to alert them. He yanked the phone back out.

THAT'S NOT WILSON NEWMAN!
THE REAL WILSON NEWMAN HASN'T BEEN SEEN SINCE HE BOARDED HIS BOAT TO COME GET YOU.

Anthony froze. If the man who'd rescued them from the island wasn't Wilson Newman, then who was he? How had he gotten his hands on the other man's badge, gun, boat and cell phone? Had he also stolen his RCMP jacket and hat? Where was the real Constable Newman?

Was he even still alive?

His body tensed to act, even before his mind could figure out how he was going to take the fake Wilson down without risking Tessa's life. After all, the man who'd called himself Wilson had a gun.

Then suddenly he felt the full force of Tessa's eyes lock on his face. He saw in an instant that somehow she knew the man she was having a bizarre chat with right now wasn't Constable Wilson Newman. What's more, she was goading the man, testing him, trying to get the fake Wilson to confess something, on camera with Zablocie and the RCMP watching.

Two words formed silently on Tessa's lips as she looked into Anthony's eyes.

Trust. Me.

Trust her? His head shook. Couldn't Tessa see what a dangerous and stupid game she was playing?

Help me, Lord. What do I do?

He texted his sister rapidly.

Send help. Backup. Now.

In the meantime, he had to keep things calm and make sure Tessa was safe until they arrived. The message spun but didn't go through.

"Obviously Drew Roberts was one of the men on the island," Tessa told the fake Wilson. Her voice was casual, almost airy, but Anthony could feel an iron sword moving through it. The fake Wilson seemed preoccupied with whatever he was looking at on his phone, but Anthony could tell he was listening.

"How'd you figure that?" Wilson asked. He took a step closer to her. But he still hadn't stepped into the camera's video.

"Well, you were attacked by the man in the green mask, right?" Tessa asked. "Big guy. Your size. He stabbed you."

Out of view. Where Anthony and Tessa had been only able to hear the ruckus.

"He was wearing this big fake prosthetic nose under his green mask," Tessa said and tapped the end of her nose for emphasis. "Not to mention a dark wig with a red bandana."

Just like the red bandana the fake Wilson had bound his cut with. A shallow cut that looked far worse than it actually was. Fake-Wilson's face paled to an ugly, ashen gray.

"That's ridiculous," he spluttered. "I saw that guy when he jumped me. His mask came off and everything. It wasn't that guy."

"Well, you were pretty focused on fighting him off," Tessa said. "He attacked you. Multiple men attacked you. You were just defending yourself while trying to escape."

And just like that, Anthony watched as Wilson relaxed again.

"Yeah," he said.

"Seriously, leaping right down the rocks the way you did instead of trying to find a safer route took major guts."

"It did."

Color began to return to his face.

"The whole thing from start to finish was really brave," Tessa added.

"Yeah," Fake-Wilson agreed. His chest rose slightly. "It was."

Tessa murmured and nodded, but she didn't reply. Instead, she left a long empty pause, which, after a moment, Wilson began to fill with a retelling of how he'd heroically survived the fight and escaped the island. The whole story was a lie. Anthony saw it now. Standing in front of him was a man who on some level desperately wanted to believe he was braver than he actually was.

But what shocked Anthony even more was how Tessa was silently encouraging the story out of him, one word at a time, as Wilson slowly walked himself into a trap of his own making, where he'd have no choice but to tell the truth to escape.

The plan might've been for Tessa to be the one on the hot seat. Instead, she was now interrogating Wilson, with such skill that he didn't even realize it.

Part of Anthony knew he should step in and take charge of the room. But another part of him wanted to see where Tessa was going with this and what she'd get Wilson to admit. If he cut her off now, would Wilson clam up? Would it take even longer to get to the truth?

For that matter, why wasn't Zablocie stepping in and ending this? His boss had to be watching it. Was he also waiting to see where Tessa was going? Would this change Zablocie's mind about Tessa being a suspect?

"I hear you," Tessa said, as Wilson's story began to wind down. "Maybe you're right that the man in the green mask wasn't Drew Roberts. After all, he was a scrawny kid, and the man in the green mask was a big, muscular guy. A serious threat. Then again, people change over time. People do bulk up. And Drew's a failed actor, right? So he'd know about stuff like costumes and disguises."

She leaned back in her chair and glanced at the laptop's camera.

"You guys won't believe the dirt I've gathered on Drew Roberts," she went on. "Real bad and messy personal stuff he wouldn't want getting out. Maybe after all this is done I'll take it to the press. Put his private life and history on blast, like people did with Cassidy."

Now Fake-Wilson's complexion began going red, like a metal pot heating to a boil. She'd suddenly started baiting him and trying to make him lose his temper. Warning bells began to ring in the back of Anthony's mind. He'd never liked it when cops used that tactic.

"I can tell you why Drew got fired from so many acting jobs," Tessa said, "and the rumors about how he treated other people on set. Especially interns. I've got financial records, employment records and witness statements—"

"Stop it!" Fake-Wilson shouted. "You can't just go around ruining a man's life by spreading lies about him!"

"Like you didn't do a fool thing to stop people from spreading lies about my friend Cassidy, after you let her die!" Tessa snapped. "You tried to kidnap me and Anthony, didn't you? Then you faked being Wilson Newman."

"So what?" he shouted. "I never hurt anyone like you're trying to say I did!"

"You let Cassidy die!" Tessa shot back. "Did you kill her, Drew?"

Suddenly Fake-Wilson/Drew Roberts lunged at Tessa with such force her chair flew back, and she tumbled to the ground. Her head cracked against the floor. He stood in front of the camera. His face filled the screen. "I didn't kill Cassidy!"

A whimper slipped from Tessa's lips and Anthony started to go toward her, but Drew pointed the gun at him.

"Don't move or I'll shoot!" he shouted.

The fall had knocked the air from her lungs, and she was struggling to breathe. Regret swept over Anthony like a flood. Yes, she'd gotten Drew to blow his cover on camera in front of Zablocie. But Anthony shouldn't have let it go so far. He should've stepped in and stopped her when she'd turned from playing good cop to bad. Again, he wondered why Zablocie had kept watching too, and if his boss's silence meant he condoned her tactics.

But, Lord, even if my boss is okay with what just happened, I'm not. This isn't who I am. This isn't how I interrogate people. Tessa baited him into losing his temper, I didn't step up and stop her and now she's hurt.

"I believe you," Anthony said quickly. "We just all need to calm down."

Anthony took a step toward the agitated man. Drew yanked his gun and aimed it again at where Tessa lay winded on the floor.

"Not another step!" Drew repeated. "Or I'll kill her! Right here and now."

EIGHT

Stars swam before Tessa's eyes. Pain radiated through her body. She gasped to take a deep and proper breath, but her aching lungs could barely sip the air. The man they now knew was Drew Roberts stood over her, bellowing threats. The gun waved wildly in front of her face. With his free hand he checked his phone. He was agitated and uncertain. She'd suspected she'd be able to goad him into admitting he was Drew, but she hadn't prepared for this.

"Now, here's what's going to happen," Drew shouted, and his voice seemed to ricochet through her brain. "I'm going to give you the address to an encrypted dark web internet portal. You're going to open up the portal and input the location of your online database into Cassidy's disappearance. Got it?" He slammed his phone down on the table with the screen up beside Anthony's laptop. His finger jabbed at the screen. "Go to this online address and give it full access to your database. Now! Otherwise something bad is going to happen."

She wondered if he knew what he was asking for. Handing over access to her entire database to a stranger online meant they could do anything with it. Change it. Delete it. But it would also make the thief vulnerable to being traced, especially considering they were still on camera and linked to the RCMP.

"Okay," she said, surprised to hear how weak her own words sounded.

She gritted her teeth and forced herself to stand. All right, so nothing had gone as planned. But still, Drew had revealed himself on camera, and they'd be able to trace who she was allowing to hack her database. Before she'd stepped into the room, something inside Tessa's heart had tried telling her not to challenge Wilson/Drew alone and that she had to find a way to let Anthony know. Maybe even let him take the lead. But at the same time a different voice in the back of her mind had told her she had to do it alone, that she couldn't fully trust Anthony or anyone else. After all, it was her life and freedom on the line.

"Let me help her, please." Anthony's voice swam at the corner of her mind.

Concern flooded his voice, and just like that her attempt at telling herself that she'd made the right choice disintegrated inside her. She knew without a doubt that, while there had been two voices arguing inside her mind, pulling her in opposite directions, she'd listened to the wrong voice.

"No!" Drew shouted. "You stay there!"

But Anthony didn't stop trying, even negotiating with Drew to let him walk over and help Tessa. Hearing the worry in his voice somehow hurt even more than the physical pain pulsating through her body. The words Anthony had whispered to her when they'd been first kidnapped back on the beach flickered in her memory. *I think I can get through to the one in the green mask.* Could he have? Could he still? She'd stabbed Lewis in the leg with a tent peg and caused them to fall off the boat before he could try.

She felt a rough hand on her arm as Drew pushed her toward the laptop. Her legs banged against the table. Drew stood close behind her and hemmed her in. He pressed the gun to the back of her head. Her own terrified face filled the screen. A string of numbers and letters appeared on the phone display. It was gibberish, and there was no way to tell what the address led to. She opened the online portal with slow deliberate keystrokes, reading each letter and number out loud to herself, hoping that somewhere on the other end of the computer's video stream an RCMP tech would be able to duplicate it and track down who was behind it.

How long had it been since the RCMP had first realized she and Anthony were in danger? How long would it take a rescue team to get there? Then a terrifying thought struck her mind—what if somehow the RCMP weren't watching? What if something had happened to the video feed, and they were all alone and no rescue was coming?

The address opened to a plain black screen that showed nothing but a white blinking box, which she typed the online location of her Cassidy Chase database into. For a second nothing happened. Then the letters blinked, the main page of the database flashed on her screen, there was a loud beep and it went black.

"Okay," she said. "It's done."

But what she didn't tell him was that it wasn't the only copy she had of her database. There were four backup copies stored on various other servers online, not to mention the physical one on her laptop at home. Then it hit her—the masked men had taken her house keys.

"Okay, Drew, you've gotten what you wanted." Anthony's voice came from somewhere behind her. It was calm and authoritative and made her think of a lighthouse beacon cutting through a storm. "I've been watching you from the beginning. You said it yourself, back on the beach. You don't want to kill anybody. You're not a bad guy. The fact you insisted that Lewis couldn't kill me might actually be the only reason I'm alive right now, and I honestly thank you for that."

She felt Drew step back far enough that she could actually turn around. And what she saw in Anthony's eyes made her breath catch in her chest—compassion. He wasn't just worried for her and determined to get her out alive. He genuinely wanted to help Drew, as well.

Hot tears filled her eyes.

Lord, I don't know where Anthony gets the heart to see people the way he does or have compassion on criminals. But please, help him, strengthen him and guide him. I really want Anthony to be right.

"You were just a kid when Cassidy disappeared," Anthony said. She heard the wooden creak as Anthony took a step forward. "You were an intern at that camp, and you'd just turned sixteen. Everybody else in the cottage that weekend was older and bigger than you. If something bad happened and you got caught up in it, you don't have to let it define your whole life."

Now Drew backed up farther until he was off camera again and standing at the side of the room where he'd been when he and Tess had first started talking. He still had the gun raised in his hand with the barrel pointed at Tessa, but his gaze darted around the room from her, to the floor, to the computer and back again, as if he was desperately trying to avoid Anthony's gaze.

"It's never too late to do the right thing and to be the person who you know you are on the inside," Anthony said. "I will help you. I promise. So, come on, man. Just put the gun down and let's get your life started back in the right direction."

Drew's hand slipped from the trigger. Slowly his hands began to rise. The gun dangled from his fingertips.

A loud banging shook the door, like the person on the outside was trying to knock it down by force. Had the police finally arrived? Was a rescue team finally here? Instinctively, Anthony stepped toward Tessa and Drew, as if positioning himself to shield them both if somebody burst through.

"Sergeant Anthony Jones!" he called. "RCMP Major Crimes—"

Before he could finish, a gunshot sounded. The bullet splintered the door.

The door flew open.

It was the man in the white mask.

The masked man raised his gun at Anthony and fired again. Anthony dropped to the ground and rolled. The bullet struck Anthony's laptop, and the screen exploded. In a swift motion, Anthony leaped to his feet, grabbed a chair and hurled it at the masked man, catching him squarely in the jaw.

It had only bought them seconds of time, but seconds was all Anthony needed.

In a single step, Anthony reached Tessa's side. He swept her up into his arms and ran for the balcony. Another shot sounded, and the sliding glass door shattered in front of them as a bullet ripped through it. Behind him he could hear the man in white shouting at Drew to do something. Anthony didn't hesitate. He ran through the broken glass, even as it caved in around them. He leaped up. His foot brushed the balcony railing. He clutched Tessa tightly to him, she tucked her head to his chest and then he jumped down off the balcony into the forest below.

He fell through the air for an instant with Tessa still tight in his arms. His boots struck the ground with such force when he landed that he stumbled forward a couple steps and nearly dropped her. But his grip remained firm.

Then, in the din of chaos and yelling, he heard Drew shout three words that seemed to rise above the noise "—just wants Tessa!"

Well, whoever wanted Tessa wasn't about to get their hands on her. Not while he had anything to say about it. Anthony turned and ran down the side of the building toward where his truck was parked.

"Okay if I just carry you for now?" he said. "I really don't want to stop to put you down."

"Fine by me."

Shouting and gunfire sounded behind them. He sprinted faster, sticking close to the side of the building and under the relative shelter of the balconies.

"Are you okay?" he asked.

"Yeah," she said. He could feel her breath on his face. "Woozy and sore, but I'm fine. You okay?"

"I am."

And he'd be even better when they were safely inside his truck.

He reached the small parking lot, thankful to hear the click of the door's remote unlocking system as he grew closer. He stopped by the passenger door, set her down and opened it for her. She tumbled in, and he practically dove across the hood to his side. A second later he was in the driver's seat. The engine started. Their doors slammed shut and locked.

"Seat belt on?"

"Yup," she called.

He started driving. They pulled out of the parking lot, cut through Princess's Main Street and then out onto a backroad. Moments later they were on a small unpaved rural road that cut through towering trees. It wouldn't be the smoothest ride or straightest drive, but it kept them off the main road, would get them back to Vancouver and was nothing his truck couldn't handle.

"So much for hoping we'd never have to do that again," Tessa said.

"The running from bullets part?" he asked. "Or my carrying you?"

"Those too," she said. "But I was thinking specifically of going over the balcony, and you did it without a harness like I did."

The road wound higher. They were driving along a tall cliff, and he could see the water of the Georgia Strait down below on his right.

"Where are you going?" she asked.

"I don't know," he admitted. "I haven't thought that far ahead yet." He glanced to the rearview mirror. There was nobody there. "Doesn't look like we're being followed." He frowned. "I need to call Zablocie and my sister. But first, I want to get my head on straight about what just happened. Did you hear what Drew shouted before we ran?"

She shuddered a breath. "Just wants Tessa?"

"Yeah, I heard that too," he said. But who wanted Tessa? And why? "How did Violet know that the man who rescued us wasn't Wilson Newman?"

Tessa's cheeks flushed.

"I called her on my laptop from the other room," she admitted. "I was feeling flustered and wanted to talk to someone about the case. She showed me a photo of the real Constable Newman, and I knew right away it wasn't him."

He felt his jaw clench. Tessa should have told him this immediately. But what had happened was in the past and fighting about it now wouldn't exactly help matters.

"Did you tell Violet?" he asked.

"I did," she said. "I told her that I'd tell you."

But Violet must've suspected Tessa wouldn't do it right away and called Anthony. She might've even alerted Zablocie.

"I'm sorry," Tessa added. "I know I should've told you. But I honestly believed I only had one shot at getting him to confess who he was, and I didn't want to risk tipping him off or something going wrong."

"But how did you know he was Drew?" he asked.

"I guessed."

He glanced at the rearview mirror again. The road was empty and silent. His hands tightened on the steering wheel.

"It's far too quiet," he said. "I know it'll take a good long while for RCMP to get out here, and local police might want to wait until they arrive. But it's been a good fifteen minutes since Drew dropped the act and threatened you. I would've expected we would be able to hear helicopters by now and maybe even start to see some action by local police. I don't understand Zablocie's actions in all this. He knew we were in trouble. The RCMP saw the whole thing unfolding on video. At least, the video had been running when you sat down and started talking to Drew, and nobody sent backup?"

He pulled the phone out of his jacket pocket and handed it to Tessa.

"Call Violet, please," he said, "and let her know we're safe. You'll find her name saved at the top of my contacts. Area code 788."

"Got it," she said.

He watched as she opened a window on his phone and hit the top number. She put it on speakerphone and turned the volume up to full so he could hear it too. But instead of the tell-tale ringing sound or his sister's voice, he just heard an odd and dull beeping sound.

"The call failed," she said.

"Okay," he said. "Then call Zablocie, put it on speaker and let me do the talking. His number is the most recent one that's called me, and the area code is 604."

She hit the button. The same three beeps sounded. A chill ran down his spine. What was happening? She dialed another number, and the same three beeps sounded. Then another, with the same result. Then her fingers moved across the screen and finally the sound of a ringing phone filled the truck.

Thank you, God, he prayed silently.

There was a click. But instead of hearing his sister's voice, he heard Tessa's:

Hello, you've reached private investigator Tessa Watson of The Chase Agency. Whoever you are and whatever you're going through, there is hope and there are people who can help you. Please leave a detailed message with your name and contact details at the tone. And if I can't take your case I'll direct you to someone who can help you.

Anthony looked over at her, confused.

"What just happened?" he asked. "You called yourself?"

"To double check if the phone was working," she said. "I couldn't get through to either your sister, Commissioner Zablocie or the RCMP headquarters in Vancouver. All the lines are down."

His head shook as his brain tried to process what she was saying. It wasn't like the RCMP's office landlines hadn't gone down before. But it was incredibly rare—maybe once a decade or so—and normally due to serious damage to the phone lines during an extreme winter storm.

"Then try my sister on her cell phone," he said. "That won't be impacted by whatever's happening to the landlines."

"I did," she said. He glanced at her. She was pale. "Twice. When I couldn't get through on either number I figured there must be something wrong with this phone—"

"So you called your office number to double-check," he finished the thought for her. "But you were able to get through. Which means both my sister's cell phone and her office landline went down at the same time."

"Yup," she said, "and your boss and team at the RCMP."

He blew out a hard breath. It felt like he'd suddenly just been punched in the gut.

"Something tells me that can't be a coincidence," he said.

Tessa was silent for a long moment. Her fingers moved across the phone's screen. Then she gasped.

"I started checking news websites," she said. "Apparently the RCMP's Vancouver headquarters suffered a major cyberattack about twenty minutes ago. Both the internet and phone lines are down. Judging by the times in the article, your boss lost internet access only a couple of minutes after I sat down. The exchange with

Drew wasn't recorded, including his confession. Neither was the internet address of the portal I gave access to my database to. Nobody knows what happened or that we're in trouble."

"Either we're dealing with someone who has very impressive technological abilities—"

"Or someone with the ability to hire a dark web criminal," she interjected.

"Yes, or they've actually got someone inside the RCMP," he said. "Maybe even within the Cassidy Chase investigation. Either way, any contact with law enforcement could be compromised. So, we don't go back to Vancouver right now or Whistler. Not while the police may be compromised and not until we know what's going on."

But where could they go? Who would help them now?

He needed to find somewhere safe where they could regroup and he could contact his sister.

"It was all for nothing," Tessa said. Her voice rose. "I goaded Drew into a fight. I got him to step in front of the camera and admit to who he was. And nobody saw any of it!"

"Hey, it's okay," Anthony said. He reached across the car with his right hand, took hers and squeezed it tightly. "It's a setback, nothing more. You and I now know the truth about two of the men who attacked us on the island. We'll figure out the third and figure out how Cassidy died."

She didn't answer for a long minute. Instead, her hand tightened in his.

Help me, Lord. I don't know what this threat is that we're dealing with or how I'm going to find justice. Who has the power to even do something like this? But I care about Tessa so much, and I want to keep her safe.

For a long moment they both looked out through the windshield at the empty road ahead of them as it twisted and turned between the trees and the rocks.

Then she pulled her hand away.

"How can you be so calm about this?" she said. "Why aren't you angry with me for going after Drew without consulting you?"

"I'm frustrated," he admitted. "Don't get me wrong, I was incredibly impressed at how you got him to confess. You're a good investigator. But I think you made the wrong call. I wish you'd trusted me."

He wished he knew how to get her to trust him.

A sudden motion in the rearview mirror caught his eye. He glanced up. A large white

delivery van was coming up the road behind them. It was driving recklessly, swerv-
ing back and forth across the center lane and
speeding far above the speed limit. The van
was coming up on them fast. The man in the
white mask was at the wheel. He had a masked
Lewis Fowler with him. Anthony glanced at
the speedometer. The turns were so tight that
if he increased his speed he'd be at risk of running off the road.

But if he didn't speed up they were going to
smash right into him.

"Hang on," he said. "We have company, and
things are going to get rocky."

NINE

"I don't know how they found us," he said, "and that worries me. I took a pretty obscure road as opposed to the main one out of town."

The road they were on wasn't even paved. His eyes darted to the rearview mirror. As much as he hated to consider it, maybe someone was tracking his phone. Considering someone had hacked the RCMP headquarters, it wouldn't be that hard to figure out what number he'd called in on. The passenger window opened, and a masked Lewis hung his head out the window for a second before pulling it back in.

Tessa turned around in her seat and looked over her shoulder.

"I can only see two of them," she said. "No Drew. Maybe he's hiding in the back of the van or maybe you actually got through to him."

Or maybe, Anthony thought, he'd actually tried to do the right thing and they'd killed him.

"They haven't started trying to shoot," Tessa said. "Yet. You think that's a good thing?"

She turned back around in her seat.

"A lack of bullets flying our way is always a good thing," Anthony said. "I'd like to say they're figuring out how to actually aim and hit their target considering how narrow and winding this road is. Except that Lewis seems like a guy who doesn't worry about aim."

His eyes darted from the road ahead to the rearview mirror and then back to the road. The van was inching closer.

"Then again, there are no hunting supply stores between here and either Whistler or Vancouver," he said. "It's not big game hunting season. You can't legally hunt anything bigger than a turkey or a rabbit right now, and you can't buy ammo without a Possession and Acquisition License. They may actually be running out of bullets with no way to refresh their stash."

No harm in looking on the bright side while also preparing for the worst.

"My guess is they're going to try to run us off the road," he said. "Did you happen to figure out who the man in the white mask is or discover anything about him that I can use to my advantage?"

"No," she said. "I searched my files but didn't get anywhere. My guess is it has to be Tom Groff or Cole Rook, as they were both at the cottage with Cassidy that weekend too. But why there were five people with her that night and only three masked assailants, I can't begin to guess."

"I'm sorry," he said. "I just realized I forgot to ask about the fact that they got ahold of your database. Does that mean that you've lost it?"

"Maybe," she said. "I don't know. Hopefully not. I'll fill you in after we get away from these guys."

Anthony pressed his foot on the gas and urged his truck as far past the speed limit as he dared. The van dropped back. But only a little. Gravel spun beneath his tires. The road was growing rougher. Anthony's vehicle was faster and more powerful. But something told him the men pursuing them were willing to drive a lot more dangerously and recklessly than he was ready to. And if they did start shooting, he wouldn't be able to drive fast enough to outrun a bullet.

He turned a corner and suddenly a vehicle appeared ahead on the road. A low and old-fashioned station wagon was coming toward him, towing a pop-up camper on the hitch.

There were an elderly couple and three kids inside the car.

Lord, help us!

The road wasn't wide enough for both of them. He swerved hard to the right, where a thin barrier of trees was all that separated them from plunging over the edge of the cliff and down into the water below. Pine needles screeched along the side of his truck, and branches buffeted against them. The car flew past so close that if Anthony had stretched his hand out the window he'd have been able to fist-bump the approaching driver's shoulder. Then the car and camper were past him and Anthony looked up to the rearview mirror to watch as the white van drove headlong toward them.

Save them, Lord. They're going to crash.

The van swerved back and forth across the road, forcing the car to drive dangerously close to the rock face on its right. The car horn blared loudly. The two vehicles flew nearer. The car swerved. The camper's back bumper smacked against the rock. The van's side mirror struck the top of the car's frame and snapped off. Then the vehicles drew apart again, and the station wagon disappeared down the road.

Anthony let out a hard breath.

Thank You, God. Please fill the people in the car with Your peace, and calm the fear in their hearts.

He hadn't realized how much he'd slowed his speed until it was too late. Suddenly the van lurched forward and clipped the truck's back bumper. Anthony and Tessa's bodies jolted forward and smacked against their seatbelts, before being tossed back against their seats. Pain shot through his body. He pressed the accelerator, and the truck surged forward again.

"You okay?" He glanced at Tessa. Her eyes were closed, and her forehead was wrinkled. She was thinking or praying, he thought, or both. Then she opened her eyes again.

"I know somewhere safe we can go," she said. "It's off the grid. No one will find us there, and we can regroup. But you'll have to disable your phone so we can't be tracked."

"Okay," he said. Turning it off and removing the battery should be enough to make it untraceable, considering it had been locked safely in his truck and nobody had touched it but him. "Where are we headed?"

"You have to turn around and drive north."

"You've got to be kidding!" His voice rose in disbelief. "The road is way too narrow. We're kicking up gravel. The van is three car lengths behind me. There are no side roads in sight. I've got a rock face wall on my left and a sheer drop to my right. And you want me to somehow turn around?"

"Yes," she replied.

He meant the question rhetorically. She'd seen how close they'd come to nearly colliding with the car and camper.

"It's impossible."

"I don't believe that," she said.

"What about this whole situation makes you think there's any way I can turn this truck around?"

Once again he was being rhetorical and wasn't expecting an answer.

"Because you're Sergeant Anthony Jones," she said firmly. Determination filled her voice and seemed to radiate into his core. "I know you can do anything you put your mind to. Now what do you need from me?"

An unfamiliar warmth moved through his body, sending fresh strength pouring through his limbs. Tessa believed in him. She knew with every fiber in her being that he could do the near impossible and somehow that was enough. How had he ever let himself forget how much she'd meant to him? How would he ever get over missing her once she was gone?

"Well, obviously I'm going to need a wide path of road," Anthony said. "Somewhere I have a hope of turning around without smashing into a rock or tree or flying off a cliff."

A sharp turn lay ahead. He gritted his teeth, tapped the brake lightly and spun the wheel. They swerved around the corner. Moments later the van was back on his tail. The passenger window rolled down, and Lewis leaned out again. Something long and metallic shone in his hand. Anthony sucked in a sharp breath. It was a baseball bat.

"We need distance," he said, "and fast. We can't let them get close enough to use that thing."

Tessa turned around and looked in the back of his cab.

"What have you got back there?" she asked.

He thought for a split second.

"Some gym equipment," he said, "and my coaching bag for my basketball team."

"Got it," she said and unbuckled her seatbelt.

"What are you doing?" he asked.

She climbed between the seats and into the back.

"Finding a way to make distance," she said. He heard the seatbelt click as she settled into the seat behind him. "What's in this little leather bag? Feels heavy."

"My bowling ball and shoes," he said. "I'm in the RCMP Canadian five-pin bowling league."

He heard the sound of his large coaching bag unzipping and then the window rolling down.

"One distraction coming right up," she said.

She began to pull basketballs out of his bag and lob them out of the window one by one. They bounced and rolled down the road. He watched as the van slowed down and swerved to avoid them. It would've almost been funny if their lives hadn't been on the line.

He crested a hill, looked down and saw his opportunity. A wide and flat swath of gray rock lay ahead on the right, like a lookout over the water. It was long and large enough that eight cars could park comfortably, and one could do a sharp U-turn in a pinch.

"Okay, I've found a place," he said. "It's not that big, but I don't want to wait to find another one. I suggest you get back in the front, so you've got an airbag if anything goes wrong."

Tessa scrambled back into the front seat. Her seatbelt clicked again, and he was vaguely aware there was something tucked under her arm, but he couldn't tell what it was. Then he heard the sound of her prayers tumbling quietly from her lips. He fixed his sight on the patch of rock ahead and prayed he'd make the turn. It would be tight, and it wouldn't be easy. But it was doable.

The patch of rock grew closer. He aimed straight for it and steered the nose of his truck toward the water. He waited for the last possible moment. His front tires crossed the rocks. He yanked the steering wheel hard. The vehicle swung wildly. Water, trees, rocks and sky blurred before his eyes. He felt his back right tire catch air as it flew out over the edge. He clenched his jaw and prayed. But somehow he stayed on the ground. Then they were back on the gravel. The vehicle righted itself. They drove up the hill heading back the way they came.

"Thank you, God," she said.

"Amen," he said.

But the danger wasn't over yet. He looked up to see the white van now flying down the road toward him. Any moment now and he'd be head-on with the men chasing them. The white van grew closer. The back door slid open. Lewis leaned out and steadied the baseball bat in one hand. They weren't going to drive straight into them. They were going to take out Anthony's windshield.

"I'm going to try to swerve around them, but I might not make it," he said.

"Roll your window down," Tessa shouted, "and keep the truck on the road."

"What are you going to do?"

"Something stupid. But it might keep them from hitting us."

He heard her seatbelt unclick. He rolled down the window. She leaned toward him. Then he saw something red and white in Tessa's other hand. It was his Canadian five-pin bowling ball. A third the size of a ten-pin bowling ball, it sat in her hand like an oversized softball. She lobbed it out the window. The van braked and swerved so hard it spun. The ball hit the pavement, split off a chunk, bounced up and smashed headlong into the van's front grill. Anthony swerved, barely coming within an inch of hitting the bumper of the van as it spun. The vehicle hit the rocks and came to a stop.

Tessa flopped back in her seat and buckled her seatbelt again.

"They're okay," she said. "I can see both men getting out of the van. I don't think either of them are injured."

Thank you, God.

He'd never killed anyone and was thankful today wasn't the day he was forced to take a life.

He kept driving up the hill and back through the woods. He could feel his heart pounding in his chest. Eventually he saw a patch of trees to his right, in between two outcroppings of rock. He pulled over, stopped the truck and switched on the hazard lights to warn any approaching vehicle they were parked at the side of the road. Then he undid his seatbelt, Tessa did too, and together they turned around and looked back. The white delivery van was a tiny, toy-sized shape far below him on the highway. It didn't look like the van would be moving again any time soon.

"That was incredibly stupid," he said.

"I told you it would be," she said. Her voice was breathless. He chuckled. "I also told you that you could do it."

"You did." He turned toward her. Her cheeks were flushed. Joy danced in her eyes. She was gorgeous, and suddenly his heart lurched with the memory of just how much he'd once longed to make her his wife. His head shook.

"Tessa, you are the bravest, gutsiest and most impossible person I've ever met and I…"

His words froze on his lips. He was unable to let himself even think of how to end the sentence. Instead, he reached for her face and slid his fingers up into her hair. She grabbed ahold of his shirt and pulled him to her.

And for a fleeting moment, their lips met.

For one sweet and tender fraction of a second, Tessa felt her world freeze as Anthony's lips brushed hers. His hands caressed the back of her head. Her fingers clutched at his shirt. But all too quickly her mind started whirling again.

What was she doing? What were they doing?

They couldn't let this happen. Solving Cassidy's murder was too important. Anthony was the only person she could well and truly count on to do it. She wouldn't let him compromise the case.

As quickly as they'd touched, they sprung apart again and retreated to opposite sides of the truck, as if they'd been hit with a volt of electricity.

"Tessa," Anthony started. "I'm… I'm sorry…"

He trailed off as words failed him. Her hand shot up.

"You don't need to say anything," she said. "In fact, it'll be less awkward if you don't. I know what you're going to say." *Or what you should say.* "You are a police officer, and I'm a suspect. You've got a case to solve, and you can't let any weird interpersonal nonsense get in the way. You have to maintain your professional integrity. Whatever just happened between us was accidental and wrong, and we can't let it happen again. Right?"

He didn't answer for a long moment. Instead, as she watched, he rolled his jaw slowly, as if sifting through his words. Suddenly she became very aware of the ticking sound of the hazard lights, and the way the rocks ahead grew red, then back to gray, then back to red again under their glare.

"Um, yeah," Anthony said. "Something like that."

"Okay, then," she said. "Is it all right if I input the coordinates to where we're headed in the GPS?"

"Sure."

She leaned forward and typed the address for one of her citizen detective friends into his truck's dashboard display screen. Then she leaned back. Wordlessly, he switched his cell phone off, pulled the battery out and slid it into his pocket. They buckled up, and he drove off, following the dot on the screen. The GPS said it was forty minutes away. She leaned back against the seat. An odd silence spread out between them. Neither of them spoke for a long moment.

"So, where am I going?" he said.

"I belong to a small, close-knit group of citizen detectives," she said. "We call ourselves the J. J. Does. We aim to keep it anonymous. First names only. But one of them has a cottage northeast of here. I'm not really allowed to tell you about him, but I'm looking forward to introducing you."

Anthony took a deep breath.

"Look, Tessa," he said. "I don't want to give you the wrong impression about what just happened between us—"

"It's fine," she cut him off. "We don't need to talk about it."

Couldn't he tell how hard she was trying to change the subject?

"You're an amazing person," Anthony said and his voice rose. "Okay? The fact that I can't let myself get too close to you, let alone ever hold you like that again, doesn't mean I don't see how incredible you are. Any man in the entire world would feel blessed beyond their wildest dreams to have you in their life. I don't know why you're so hard on yourself. And why you can't see yourself the way God does and the way I do. Maybe it has something to do with your parents—"

"I did something my parents say is unforgivable," she interjected.

Anthony stopped.

"I'm so sorry," he said. "I can't imagine you ever doing anything that's unforgivable."

Hot tears pressed to the back of her eyes.

"You know those DNA tests you can get where you mail them in and they send you your results?" she asked. He nodded. "Well, they can be a game changer when it comes to solving crimes, especially cold cases. A lot of people load their results online to find unknown relatives. But those same online databases can be used to identify unknown bodies or track down killers. Some really major crimes have been solved that way."

She took a deep breath and steeled herself for the next part of the story. Anthony's right hand slid off the steering wheel and began to reach across the front of the cab for hers. But then he stopped himself, pulled back and gripped the steering wheel with both hands.

"I took a DNA test," she went on. "I just believe in the power of crowdsourced data and wanted to add mine online. Figured I might find some interesting third cousins." She shuddered a breath. "Instead, I discovered my dad's not my biological father."

Something seemed to break behind Anthony's eyes. His hand shot across the seats again. This time he grabbed hold of Tessa's hand and held it tightly. She squeezed his hand back, and for a long moment neither of them said anything. Then he pulled away.

"I'm so sorry," he said.

"I didn't know what to think," she said. "My parents always held themselves up as an example of perfection. They always told me they'd been dating since they were teenagers and never so much as kissed before they got married. I was upset, but I was also curious, even compassionate. It made me feel like they were real and human people. I even hoped finding out the truth would bring us closer. So, I sat them down, told them about the DNA results and asked them about it."

"And?" Anthony asked.

"They denied it," she said. "Very angrily. They told me the DNA results were a total lie. They said they'd never been so insulted and demanded I apologize to them. They haven't spoken to me since." She took a deep breath and blew it out. "I took the test three times with three different companies. They all gave the same result. I'm an investigator. I want to know the truth, and they're angry at me for even asking."

"They might be embarrassed or ashamed," Anthony said gently. "It could also be a bad memory that they've tried very hard to forget. Or even a traumatic memory your mother has forgotten. Memory is a tricky thing, and shame is pretty powerful. But either way, you deserve the truth."

"And I might never get it," she said.

"Yeah," he said. Compassion flooded his voice. "You might never get it. And I'm sorry about that."

Silence fell between them again. She suspected he was waiting to see if she wanted to say anything more. But oddly there wasn't anything more she needed to say. She'd finally shared this big secret that had been eating her up inside for years, and Anthony had listened. Somehow that had been enough.

Ten minutes passed, then twenty, in a comfortable silence punctuated only by the sound of the engine humming and the tires on the road.

"We still haven't talked about your database," he said eventually.

"I'm not worried about whoever was on the

other end of that portal reading what all I've gathered," she said. "One of the big differences between private investigators and law enforcement is we don't generally have access to classified documents. Everything I've gathered is out in the open for anyone who looks hard enough. But what really worries me is the possibility of somebody deleting it. I only gave them access to my main portal. I have five other online backups, plus a stored copy on my home computer. But considering how powerful this guy is and the fact the masked men stole my house keys, it's possible they'll be able to delete all of it before we can save it."

"Hopefully that won't happen," he said.

They followed the blinking dot on the GPS deeper and deeper into the mountain, along increasingly smaller and smaller roads, until finally they were right on top of it. Anthony slowed his truck to a crawl.

"Right there," she said and pointed. "I think."

To their right lay a narrow road almost completely buried by the brush that surrounded it.

He turned the vehicle and, once they pushed past the initial crop of bushes, found a well maintained dirt road behind it. They drove down it slowly. Then a dwelling came into view, one story tall with thick log walls and a shingled roof, that looked too rustic to be called a house but too large to be called a cabin.

He pulled to a stop. Tessa opened her door first and hopped out. Anthony followed. But she'd barely heard his truck door slam shut when she heard the click of a rifle, and an elderly man stepped into view. He was over six foot five, with thick white hair and a generous beard.

Anthony's jaw dropped.

"You're General Alberto McClean," he said. "You got the Order of Canada for stopping a gunman during a session of parliament. I became a cop because of you. You were my hero."

"It's just Bert now," the man said. "Nice to finally meet you, Anthony. Tessa told me all about that essay you wrote on me when you were young." She felt herself blush. "Believe me, being a hero is not all it's cracked up to be. At least not the famous kind. The media spends your first five minutes of fame getting you built up onto some giant pedestal no man could actually inhabit, and the next ten minutes trying to tear you right back down off it."

Then he glanced past Anthony to Tessa and his scowl melted away into an almost parental smile. He lowered his weapon to his side.

"Nice to see you live and in person, Tessa," Bert said. "I'm sorry it has to be under these circumstances, but I'm glad you came to me."

"What circumstances?" Tessa asked.

How did he know she was in trouble?

"Your face is all over the news," Bert said. Concern filled his eyes. "The RCMP have got a nationwide manhunt going on for you right now. They say you're on the run from police. It's an 'if you see this person, do not try to engage, but call law enforcement immediately' kind of thing. Every news outlet in the country is saying you killed your childhood best friend."

TEN

Her thoughts raced as she and Anthony followed Bert into a generous but somehow also overstuffed living room. In fact, the entire one story somehow seemed both larger and smaller than she expected. The building itself was deceptively narrow from the outside but went much farther back in the woods than she thought. It had a huge living room—larger than her first apartment—with doors leading off to what she guessed were smaller rooms on the side. The living room was separated only by an island counter from a generous-sized kitchen, which then led to huge floor-to-ceiling windows that looked out on a large porch, more trees and a lake.

And yet, the house was also so filled with boxes, books and papers that it somehow seemed almost cramped. Overstuffed shelves filled every inch of wall. The kitchen was lined with rows of jars of food and jugs of water. And she was sure somewhere on the property she'd find a garage or shed filled with enough wood and fuel to last a lifetime.

A clock on the wall told her it was twenty after four. Seems Zablocie hadn't been joking about sending the cavalry after her if she didn't turn herself in by four. Now she wouldn't be able to so much as grab a coffee without worrying every working phone in the place was being used to report her to police.

"Well, I guess you'd better sit down and explain what all this is about," Bert said. He waved his hand toward a brown leather sofa that looked like it had been meticulously and lovingly patched by hand.

"First I need a computer with an untraceable internet portal," Tessa said. "The criminals who are after us got access to my entire database on the Cassidy Chase file and I'm worried they might've deleted it. I do have backups stored all over the web, but if they're really good they'll be able to use the main database to find those too."

Bert's white bushy eyebrows rose. "Who's after you?"

"I'll explain," Anthony said, "while Tessa tries to save her database. But first, do you have a phone I can use to contact my sister? She's a corporal with Missing Persons, and she'll be worried sick about me."

Bert walked over to a side table and pulled a phone out of the drawer. It was a bulky satellite device and as thick as six regular cell phones.

"It's untraceable," Bert said. "But the number to call you back on is written on the side."

Anthony dialed his sister's number and, when she didn't answer, left a brief message saying they were safe and to call when she could. He ended the message and offered the phone back to Bert.

"Hold on to it for now," Bert said. "You'll need it for when she calls you back."

Tessa had the distinct impression from the look on Bert's face that he wasn't the kind of person accustomed to letting people just show up at his house unannounced and take over, but that he was willing to give them a little bit of rope. For now. She wasn't sure how far that would stretch but she was thankful for it while she had it. Bert walked over to a door on the side of the room and ushered them through.

It was like walking into an alternative reality version of her own office at home. There was a sturdy desk crowded with papers, boxes of files set up against the wall, research books open on every available surface and both a laptop and desktop computer. A dozen different jerseys and sweaters swamped a rack on the back of the door. Bert went over to the desktop, jiggled the mouse to bring it to life and opened a secure dark web portal. He waved Tessa toward it. She dropped into the chair and started typing. Bert turned to Anthony expectantly.

"Now, it's time you tell me what's going on," he said. "Start at the beginning and be thorough."

"I'm a sergeant with the RCMP Major Crimes Unit's Unsolved Homicide Unit," Anthony said. "Early this morning a set of human remains were found at a cottage near Whistler. Those remains were identified as Cassidy Chase's, and it's the same cottage where she was staying with five colleagues the weekend she disappeared. A vitriolic letter from Tessa to Cassidy about Cassidy's on-again, off-again boyfriend Kevin was found on the body, which in hindsight looked like motive and was enough to have Tessa considered a person of interest. When she evaded police attempts to bring her in, I went after her. At the same time, Tessa was contacted by a pawnshop, telling her that Cassidy's bracelet had turned up on a small island off the coast of Princess."

"He knows that part," Tessa said. "I filled the group chat in this morning. Bert thought it was a trap."

"And I'm guessing I was right," Bert said.

"Very much so," Anthony said. "I followed Tessa to the island, where we were ambushed by three men with masks. We've identified two of them so far as Drew Roberts and Lewis Fowler, who were both with Cassidy when she disappeared. It appears like they're trying to kidnap Tessa, not kill her. But it's hard to tell because they're disorganized and sloppy."

Anthony continued to fill Bert in on their various run-ins with the masked men. Tessa opened the database. It was empty. Not a single document, picture or news report remained. She blew out a hard breath. Okay, that wasn't completely unexpected. She accessed her first backup database. It was empty too. She breathed a sigh when she opened the third and saw a screen full of icons, only for her relief to fade as she watched the number of icons drop in real time.

"We've got a problem," she said. "There's someone in my backups now, and they're deleting everything."

She heard footsteps on the floor, then felt Anthony behind her. His hands touched her shoulders gently, and there was something both strengthening and comforting about the simple gesture.

"What can we do?" Anthony asked. "How can we help?"

"I need to back everything up before it's gone forever," she said.

"You've got multiple backups?" Bert asked. He was already on the move toward a large metal cabinet. He pulled out a new and unopened external memory drive.

"Several," she said. "But maybe not enough. They've already deleted two and a half of them."

Bert unboxed the hard drive and plugged it into the back of his computer. "Are your backups saved in some kind of sequential order?"

"They are," she said.

"Then I suggest you go to the final one and start saving it," he said.

She went straight for the final database and opened it, thankful to see all the folders and files were still there. She highlighted them all and dragged them into the icon for the external hard drive. A progress bar appeared with the animated GIF of a sheet of paper flying like a butterfly from one side to the other. The screen predicted the copy would take over half an hour.

"How many files are we looking at?" Bert asked.

"Thousands," Tessa said.

"Unfortunately, they're probably going to be able to delete faster than we can copy," Bert said, "especially if they have a faster internet connection than we do or multiple computers going at once. Hopefully we won't lose too much."

The idea of losing even one clue into Cassidy's disappearance made her wince.

"I have an out of the box idea," Anthony said.

He highlighted the items in the reverse order and hit Ctrl P. She heard the sound of gears beginning to turn as a printer on the far side of the room sprung to life.

"You just set my entire database to print?" she asked.

"Yup," Anthony said. "In the opposite order of how things are being copied. So hopefully if our hacker does get to this database before we can save it all, we'll still have paper backups."

He was still standing behind her. She reached back and squeezed his arm.

"How old-school of you," she said. "Thank you. You never cease to amaze me."

Anthony chuckled softly. "Just as long as we don't run out of printer paper and ink."

"That won't be a problem," Bert said.

Anthony stepped back and Tessa turned. Bert was standing back against the wall with his arms crossed again, watching them both with a curious look on his face, as if he was trying to solve a puzzle even more complicated than what had happened to Cassidy.

"You'll find everything you need in that metal cabinet," he added, gesturing to a different one than the cabinet where he'd pulled the hard drive from. "And you're on printer duty, young man."

Anthony grinned. "Yes, sir."

"And, Tessa, stop staring at the screen," Bert added. "Watching the problem isn't going to solve it faster. I'd suggest we go talk in the other room because it's larger and nicer, but we should stay on the lookout for printer jams."

"Actually," Anthony said, "Tessa hasn't eaten in hours. I hate to impose on you any further, but it's important she takes care of herself."

Bert's brows knit and his quizzical look deepened.

"Yeah, I've got some chili and rolls in the freezer I can throw in," he said. He nodded to Tessa. "Come give me a hand in the kitchen. Then we'll all sit down and start making heads or tails of what's actually happening here."

She glanced at Anthony.

"Take your time," Anthony said. "I'm not going anywhere." He pulled the first batch of documents from the tray, rapped it on the table to make it straight and stacked them. She followed Bert back into the main living area and from there into the kitchen.

He fired up the wood-burning stove and pointed her in the direction of one of the two large chest freezers that sat under the island. She opened it. Inside there was enough food to last Bert years. She pulled out a baggie of chili and another that contained rolls. Both looked handmade. Bert popped the chili in a large stoneware pot on the stove, which he set to low heat, and put the buns in the oven.

"Okay, we should have food in about thirty," he said. "There are homemade granola bars in a jar on the counter if you need something to tide you over."

"Thank you," she said. She didn't have an appetite, but maybe she would when the food was ready. "I don't know where I'd be right now without you."

"No problem." He nodded. "I know you'd do the exact same for me or any other one of the citizen detectives if push came to shove. Just one thing I need to know to get my head around this. If the man busy guarding my printer is the same Anthony you told me about dating when you were younger, remind me again why you never married this guy?"

"Does that really matter?" Tessa asked.

"To getting you out of this murder charge mess you're in?" Bert asked. "Yes, I think it does."

"Because I was seventeen years old and angry," Tessa said, and suddenly she realized that was probably the most honest answer she'd ever given to that question—even when she'd been the one asking it.

Bert nodded as if she'd told him what he needed to know. "All right then."

They walked back into the office to find Anthony had started sorting the pages into multiple stacks.

Bert sat down in the office chair that Tessa had vacated and spun it around to face them both. Tessa sat on one arm of the couch opposite him.

"So, am I finally up speed?" Bert asked. "Or is there anything I'm still missing?"

"You've got all the facts," Tessa said. "But I'd add I don't think our attackers liked each other or wanted to work together. I wouldn't be surprised if they hadn't seen each other since

Cassidy's disappearance, and were forced back together by the fact her body was found."

"I have some questions," Bert said. "When did construction start at the cottage?"

"About a week ago," Anthony said.

"So, presuming Cassidy's killers—or killer and accomplices—had been keeping an eye on the property in one way or another, they knew her body was about to be found and had a little time to plan their counterattack," Bert said. "Next question. Do we have any idea what happened to the real Constable Wilson Newman?"

"Not as far as I know," Anthony said. "According to my sister, he was seen boarding his boat to head for the island. The fact his phone showed a recent call with my boss, and Drew knew all about Zablocie, makes me wonder if Wilson reached the island and his attackers overheard his call with Zablocie before taking him out."

"Or there's something very wrong inside the RCMP," Tessa added.

"If the chief superintendent of Major Crimes suspected Tessa was involved first thing this morning, why did he wait until this afternoon to name her as a suspect?" Bert said. "Why give her all day to run?"

"I talked him into giving me until four to bring her in," Anthony said. "I convinced him that bringing Tessa in as a willing witness would garner us a lot more usable information than if she was arrested or declared a suspect."

Bert's eyebrows shot up. "Really?"

"It's a common police tactic," Anthony added. He sounded defensive. "Sometimes we try to bring a suspect in for a voluntary police interview first, before issuing a warrant, in the hopes of getting them to cooperate."

"Anthony is incredibly good at his job," Tessa chimed in. "His boss had every reason to trust him. Back at the inn, he had one of the criminals ready to turn himself in, when suddenly the other one shot up the door."

"And Tessa was the one to trick him into blowing his cover," Anthony added. "Which would've worked if somebody hadn't cut the video feed."

Bert snorted. "Aren't you two quite the pair?"

A piece of paper escaped from the printer and fluttered to the ground. He bent down, picked it up and handed it to Anthony.

"Not a day passes where I don't thank the Lord that I'm no longer young," he added. "And yes, I imagine you must've been an impeachable officer with an incredible record, if you managed to talk the chief superintendent into this."

"In Anthony's defense," Tessa said, "I'm pretty headstrong, and he probably was the only one who had any hope of getting me to agree to turn myself in."

"Oh, I believe that," Bert said. "But I wouldn't have given him seven minutes, let alone seven hours."

He chuckled like he was listening to a joke that only he could hear. Then his smile faded.

"I don't blame you for not wanting to be arrested, Tessa," he added. "Once you're behind bars, police will seize every scrap of information you have on the case, and it'll be up to your lawyer to fight in court to get access to it. You're welcome to stay here tonight, but you can't just hide out here forever. You will be arrested eventually, and we get one crack at solving this case before that happens. If I have to go to bat for you once you're behind bars, I want to be armed to the teeth, and so far nothing about this case makes a lick of sense. So, tell me, who killed Cassidy?"

"I don't know," Tessa said. "I do know that Lewis and Drew were there when she disappeared and that the third masked man is probably Tom or Cole, or someone connected to Katie. But I can't see how any of them could've killed her. The timing just doesn't work."

"What about the man she was seen leaving the bar with?" Bert pressed.

"He was never identified," Anthony said. "But based on his accent and clothing, it was assumed he was a member of Italy's juniors roller-ski team, who were in Whistler that weekend. But every member of the team was on the bus and accounted for less than twenty minutes after Cassidy left the bar. Not enough time to kill someone and take them back to the cottage."

Tessa flipped to her file database on the computer. The number of documents had already started dropping. Their unseen enemy had found it and started deleting files faster than she could copy them. She just hoped Anthony's backup plan would be enough to save them all from being destroyed.

She clicked a folder, and up popped a gallery of high-definition pictures and videos she'd gleaned from social media of the team, both on the bus back to Vancouver and then on the flight home.

Bert glanced at the screen. "Somebody on that team had a stellar camera."

"Earlier we'd been trying to figure out why Cassidy would've left her colleagues and walked out of the bar with a stranger," Tessa said. "After spending a few hours being chased by them, I'd be far less surprised to find out she didn't like their company."

"On the surface this entire thing looks very random," Bert said, "but it also feels incredibly planned. Before the facts started coming out, who did you suspect killed her?"

"Her ex-boyfriend," Tessa said automatically. "Kevin Scotch-Simmonds. He was possessive and controlling, and I never liked him. But there's no way he was the man she left the bar with, and he has an alibi that puts him hours away."

Bert didn't answer. Her gaze drifted past him and Anthony to the large glass windows, which looked out on the forest beyond.

"They met about three and a half months before she died," she said. "Give or take. Cassidy was working at a donut shop, and he used to come in and flirt with her. She was seventeen. He told her that he was eighteen."

"How old was he really?" Bert asked.

"Twenty-five," Tessa said. "She'd said she wasn't really attracted to him but he was… persistent. He'd bring her gifts and offer to give her a ride home in his car. He's the kind of man who believes money can buy everything. Within three weeks she admitted that they'd started dating. Before he came along, we'd talk every day, and I'd see her several times a week. But once she met him she kind of disappeared. Then, in the middle of June…"

Her voice suddenly caught in her throat.

Anthony reached his hand across the room, grabbed her fingers and squeezed tightly. She squeezed him back.

"It was the nineteenth," Anthony supplied.

"Cassidy called me after eleven and said she was at a party with Kevin," Tessa went on. "She was crying. She said they'd gotten into a big fight and she wanted to go home, but was scared to leave. So I climbed out the window and caught a bus to go get her. My parents were very strict about curfew, so I had to sneak out. When I got there, she was hysterically upset. I told Kevin I was taking her home—"

"And Kevin hit Tessa," Anthony said. Something protective and strong moved through his voice. He still hadn't let go of her hand.

Bert's face hardened. "I'm so sorry."

"He was aiming for Cassidy, and I stepped between them," Tessa said. "I took Cassidy, and we locked ourselves in the bathroom. I called Anthony, and he came to get us."

She turned to Anthony and looked into his eyes. He'd been so brave and so strong. Barely eighteen, with nothing to his name but his integrity and his beat-up little car, but he'd walked in there, wrapped one arm around her and the other around Cassidy and led them out.

"And Kevin didn't try to stop you?" Bert asked.

"He did," Tessa said. "Kevin came out swinging and tried to tackle Anthony, but Anthony put him down on the ground without even throwing a punch."

She exhaled, as if she'd somehow been holding her breath since that night and hadn't let it out since. Then she pulled her hand away from Anthony's, and he went back to stacking papers.

"Cassidy had a pretty nasty cut," she went on. "I had a black eye, and Anthony was worried I might have a concussion. He took us to the hospital, called all our parents and called the police. But Cassidy told the police that I'd made everything up and Kevin hadn't done anything wrong. A few days later, Cassidy told me our friendship was over and blocked me on her phone, email and social media. I was upset and sent her a stupid and angry letter. I thought we'd get past it. But five weeks later, she was gone."

"And Kevin has an alibi for her death," Bert said.

"He does," Anthony said. "Now, it's no one outside his immediate family. But we also have nothing placing him in Whistler that night."

The printer screeched suddenly with a high-pitched and metallic wail. A paper had jammed. Anthony wriggled it free, but still it ripped at the edges. The printer started purring again.

Anthony looked at the page and frowned.

"What are you looking at?" Tessa asked.

"A list of all the cops who were involved in the initial search when Cassidy disappeared," he said. "I know a lot of them. At least a dozen or so are still working within the RCMP now. Including Zablocie."

"Have you tried to contact him yet?"

"No." Anthony shook his head. "I know I need to, but I haven't figured out what to say."

"Remember," Bert said. "Just because my line is secure and untraceable doesn't mean his line is secure or someone isn't tracing your call."

"Got it," Anthony said. He reached into his

jacket pocket and fished out the phone Bert had given him. She watched as cautious relief filled his face. "Apparently, I missed a callback from my sister."

"I suggest you make your calls out back," Bert said. "It's nice and quiet, plus the signal tends to be stronger."

"Will do," Anthony said. "Thanks."

He wasn't quite sure what he was going to say to his sister, but it would be good to hear her voice. He had even less idea what he was going to say to Zablocie. As far as his boss knew, Anthony had disappeared at the start of the video interrogation and taken off with the suspect.

"Can you ask Violet to drop by my place and see if anyone's let themselves in or taken anything?" Tessa asked. "I don't exactly have any valuables, but I'm worried about my laptop and computer."

"Will do," Anthony said.

She quickly ran him through how to locate the specific pale blue stone in the multicolored rock garden behind her house that had her spare key buried beneath it.

"Got it," he said with a smile. "Can you babysit the printer for me?"

"Sure thing," she said, "but to be honest, I don't think it'll be that much longer." She glanced at the screen. "The hard drive has stopped copying files. We got a little over seventy percent saved before he managed to wipe my database clean. Hopefully, the rest were saved by your printer strategy. But I'll have to sort through this mound of paper before I know for sure what we have and what we don't."

Anthony walked back into the main room. His senses were assailed with the fresh aroma of bread, tomatoes and spices. He went through the kitchen, instinctively turned the heat down on the chili as he passed, and then walked out the sliding back door. He stepped out onto a large handcrafted deck of beautiful red hardwood. Thick trees spread out around him. Straight ahead lay a dark blue-green body of water that was somewhere in size between a small lake and a large pond. Wooden steps led down to the water, with a square dock, swimming ladder and a single Adirondack chair.

He dialed his sister's number and put the phone to his ear. He hung up after one ring and called back immediately, another code they'd concocted to tell the other to hurry up and answer.

He heard the phone click and the sound of her breathing, but she didn't speak. There was a background thrumming sound that made him think she was driving.

"Vi, it's me," he said.

"Anthony, hi!" Her happy voice rang in his ear and brought a smile to his face.

"Glad to see you're being cautious," he said.

"Well, it came up as a blocked number," she said. "Where are you?"

"Safe, with Tessa and a friend," he said. "What happened? The video call was about to start and then it went down."

"Isolated outage," she said. "Internal phone lines, internet and local cell tower all went down at once."

"Cyberattack?"

"It hasn't been confirmed either way," Violet said. "But that would be my guess. It was down for over an hour."

"Did you hear Zablocie has put a warrant out for Tessa's arrest?" he asked.

"I saw the press conference," she said. "I did contact his office about the fake Constable Wilson Newman and found out the real Wilson called Zablocie after he arrived on that island."

So, his theory that the masked trio had

jumped him might be right. He started to walk down the steps toward the water.

"I need you to do something for me," he said. "I need you to get a police officer you trust, go to Tessa's house on the down-low, and see if anyone has broken in and messed with anything."

"I am a police officer, Ant," she said. With more than a slight hint of reproach in her voice.

"Yes, I know," he said quickly. "But I don't want you to get hurt."

"This is my actual job," she said. "I'm a Corporal with RCMP Missing Persons. Poking around empty houses for clues is kind of my area of expertise."

"Yes, but you're also my sister," he said, "and I'd feel better if—"

"Anthony Jones!" Violet cut him off firmly with a tone that disconcertingly reminded him of their mother. He stopped halfway down the steps. "You're my brother and I adore you, but you're also the bossiest person I know."

Bossy? He blinked. "I'm not bossy."

"You know why we always had different friends and different hobbies growing up?" she said. "Because you had to be the leader of every group we were in. You chose the game. You dictated the rules we had to play by and the roles everybody had. Right now, you are in trouble. Tessa is in trouble. For all we know the RCMP itself is in trouble. Let me do my job and help you."

Half a dozen arguments leaped to his lips. Instead, he looked out at the water and silently thanked God for his sister.

"Okay," he said. He couldn't exactly control what his sister was going to do anyway. He gave her Tessa's address and directions on how to find Tessa's key. Violet told him to stay safe and that she'd call him back. Then he clicked off and dialed his boss.

"Chief Superintendent Wade Zablocie," his boss answered immediately.

"Hi, sir, it's Anthony," he said. "Sergeant Anthony Jones."

He kept walking down the steps toward the water.

He heard his boss let out a prayer of thanksgiving under his breath.

"Good to hear your voice," Zablocie said. "We were worried when we lost communication. Are you all right?"

"I am."

"And Miss Watson? Is she with you?"

"She is."

"Where are you now?"

Anthony paused at the bottom of the steps and prayed for wisdom.

"After the video feed cut out, Tessa discovered that the man we thought was Constable Wilson Newman was actually Drew Roberts, one of the five people who were with Cassidy Chase the day she disappeared," Anthony went on as if he hadn't heard the chief superintendent's question. He talked quickly, trying to get as much information out as possible before his boss cut him off, while also knowing anything he said might be overheard by the people out to get them. "That's two of her attempted kidnappers we've identified. I don't know who the third one is, but he had a tattoo inside his wrist."

"Your sister briefed us on Mr. Roberts's and Mr. Lewis's possible involvement," Zablocie said. "Warrants have been issued for their arrest. Search and rescue are currently looking for Constable Newman."

"Then you can understand my belief that Tessa is a victim here," Anthony said. "Not a perpetrator."

"You are too good an investigator to believe that life is that binary," Zablocie said. He sounded frustrated. "Yes, we have abundant evidence that people are targeting her and have threatened her life. That does not prove that she's innocent of the crimes she's been charged with. Not by a long shot. You've investigated enough cases and turned enough suspects into cooperating witnesses to know cases can be layered and messy."

"But with all due respect—"

"I'm not going to let my prime suspect in a murder case roam free just because other people are trying to kill her." Zablocie cut him off. "Give me your location, and I'll get someone to come pick you and Miss Watson up immediately. I know you've been doing good work out there, but it's long past time we brought you in, and the longer Tessa's free, the greater risk that either she'll disappear or that something will happen to her."

"I don't really think she's a flight risk anymore," Anthony said.

"Heard," Zablocie said. "But it's not your call, and it isn't up for debate. Once you're back in the office and she is safe in custody we can discuss further options for other avenues you think the investigation should pursue. Now, send me your location, make sure you keep her in your sights and I'll dispatch rescue immediately."

Anthony took a deep breath.

"I'm afraid I can't do that, sir."

"Can't or won't?" Something hardened in Zablocie's voice.

"Won't," Anthony said sadly. And yet he was also oddly thankful his boss made him take ownership of his decision by pointing out the difference. "I don't know what's going on right now, who's after Tessa or what it has to do with the phone lines and the internet going down. And I'm not accusing anyone within the RCMP of anything untoward. I'm simply making a decision I think is in the best interest of both Tessa Watson and solving Cassidy Chase's murder."

"Then I have no choice but to charge you with disobeying orders, impeding a police investigation and aiding and abetting a suspect," Zablocie said, "and to issue a warrant for your arrest and suspend you, effective immediately, pending investigation."

"I understand, sir," Anthony said, "and my answer is still no."

"Anthony." An unexpected kindness filled Zablocie's voice. "You're a good officer, and there's no coming back from something like this. All I'm asking is that you bring her in for questioning. Just convince her to turn herself in and this all goes away, and I won't pursue charges against you. Are you sure you're willing to end your career to protect this woman?"

"I am. I'm sorry."

He ended the call, slid the phone back into his pocket and looked out over the water. His entire body felt numb in the way it did after he'd just suffered an injury but hadn't felt the pain kick in yet.

Lord, I don't even know what to pray. I've never needed You more than I do right now, and I don't even know what to say.

He heard footsteps behind him and turned to see Tessa walking down toward him. A bright light sparkled in her eyes, and he could tell she'd thought of something interesting. But as she looked into his face her smile vanished. "What's wrong?"

"My career is over," he said. "I've been suspended. I'm not really a cop anymore. I'm a criminal on the run, just like you. Zablocie gave me a choice. Either I bring you in or he'd issue a warrant for my arrest. And I chose you."

ELEVEN

"Oh, Anthony," she said. "I'm so sorry."

The pain she could see in his deep blue eyes seemed to flow into her own heart. Without thinking, she stepped forward, wrapped her arms around his waist and hugged him. Her cheek pressed against his chest. Slowly and tentatively, he wrapped his arms around her too. And for a long moment they held each other.

Sadly, she could all too easily imagine a world without Anthony in her life. But she couldn't imagine one where he wasn't working in law enforcement and doing everything in his power to fight for justice.

Lord, I never wanted Anthony to be brought down by the mess I'm in. You have to save his career. He has to be a cop. Anthony has to be okay. He can't lose it all. Not because of me. Help me. What do I do?

She pulled back just enough to look at his face, but still her hands lingered on his shoulders, and his fingers nestled against the small of her back.

"No, you have to be a cop," she said firmly, as if she was forceful enough to make it so. "It's who you are. It's what you were made to do. They can't suspend you, arrest you, label you a criminal or whatever it is they're trying to do. You have to get in your truck right now, drive to Vancouver and press your case."

"I can't," Anthony said. "I just can't."

Anthony's head shook. He took a step back and his hands began to slip from her body. But she didn't let him go.

"Yes, you can," she said. "I'll be fine. I can stay here with Bert. We can work the case here, while you go back to the RCMP and investigate it from there. I am confident that when you argue your case to the chief superintendent, you'll be able to make him see that you haven't done anything wrong—"

"Yes, I have," Anthony cut her off. "You're innocent of the charges they've levied against you. But I'm not. I'm one hundred percent guilty. I disobeyed a direct order. I aided and abetted a suspect."

"But if you go talk to him—"

"It won't make any difference," Anthony said. "Because unless you're in custody you'll still be a suspect out on the run who I helped escape. Until you're behind bars he won't listen to me, let alone give me another shot."

Understanding dawned. "So, you said when he gave you a choice, you meant that either you arrest me or he's going to arrest you?"

"Sort of," he said. "But it doesn't matter. Because I'm not gonna be the one that takes your freedom away. Not for a crime that I know you didn't commit. Giving up your active investigation into clearing your name and instead turning yourself in to police has to be your choice. Not mine. And I'm not going to make that choice for you."

She let him go. Anthony turned and walked away from her toward the end of the dock. He stared out at the water.

"Violet told me that I'm bossy," he said. "I don't know if I'd use that word. But she's not wrong. When we were kids, I always organized the games my friends and I were playing or chose the television shows. My teachers said I was an 'organizer' and a 'leader.' But that's probably because I was a boy."

"You definitely had strong opinions on things," she said. "But so do I."

"Isn't that true?" He chuckled softly. "I think we even each other out."

He turned back to face her again.

"Tessa," he said. "I'm sorry I called your folks and the police after the incident at Kevin's place without talking to you first."

"But you thought you were doing the right thing," she said, "and you probably were."

"Then I should've tried to convince you," he said. "I was wrong not to at least try. But I didn't want to argue my case or hear your opinion. I just wanted to be right. I didn't even give you the choice of making the calls yourself, or preparing yourself for their arrival or finding some other option."

She hadn't even realized she'd been walking toward him or that he'd been coming toward her, until their feet met in the middle of the dock.

He reached up and cupped the sides of her face with his hands.

"Tessa, I feel like I keep trying to tell you something and it never gets through," he said. "But you are the strongest, bravest, most independent, most intelligent person I've ever known. I don't just like you and care about you a whole lot, I respect you. I value you. I am better when I'm around you."

His eyes locked on hers, as if he was drowning and his only chance of rescue lay in her gaze. She felt her breath catch in her throat. His fingers slipped along the back of her neck and up into her hair.

"To be honest," he said, "looking back at what we did over a dozen years ago, I don't know if I was right or wrong. I don't even know that about everything that happened today. I just know that I should've honored you, better than I have. And the only thing that would hurt worse than not being able to be a cop anymore is knowing I was making the same mistake by not having your back now."

I feel the same way about you. I have to respect you and have your back too.

The words leaped to her lips. But before she could speak them, his kiss stole them away. She clutched Anthony to her, as he kissed her in a way he never had before.

This wasn't the kiss of a nervous and infatuated young man, like he'd been when they'd first found each other. Or a spontaneous kiss of relief and adrenaline, like the way they'd kissed back in his truck when they'd escaped the masked men.

No, this was the kiss of a man who knew who he was at his core and who he wanted to be.

A loud and high-pitched ringing sound shattered the quiet.

They leaped apart, and he pulled out his phone and glanced at the screen.

"It's my sister," he said. He put the phone to his ear, turned away and answered it. But he'd barely exchanged a few words with her before he turned back. "Hang on. I'm going to put you on speakerphone so we can all be in on this conversation."

"Hi, Violet!" Tessa stood beside Anthony and leaned toward the phone. "How are things going?"

"Search and Rescue found Constable Newman's body," Violet said sadly. "He was floating in the water not far from the island where you guys were. It looks like someone shot him in the back shortly after he arrived on the island to come get you."

Tessa gasped a painful breath.

"I'm so sorry," Anthony said. "Any arrests?"

"Not yet," Violet said. "But the bullets are the same caliber as the ones they found all over the island. You may have escaped fairly unscathed so far. But please know the people you're dealing with are killers. Your life is in danger."

"Did you hear I've been suspended and

they're pressing charges against me?" Anthony asked.

"Not yet," Violet said. "But I'm sure I'll be officially informed soon. In the meantime, don't tell me anything about where you are. If you need my help, know that I'll always be there for you, and I will do everything in my power to keep you safe. But I'm also going to assume I'm being watched, and they could tap my phone or trace my calls. I'll be compromised."

"Understood," Anthony said.

Tessa took a step back. A good cop had died because of her, another one had already lost his career and now another might be forced to jeopardize hers.

Lord, what can I do? How do I stop this?

"There's more," Violet said. "I'm at Tessa's house right now. I'm sorry to tell you that I can't find a laptop, desktop computer or even any electronic devices more complicated than a toaster. Someone's been here before me and taken them all."

Tessa felt her legs suddenly go weak. She sank into the Adirondack chair. Anthony slid the phone into her hand.

"They didn't just take my files on Cassidy Chase," she said. "They took everything, on every investigation I've ever done or am working on now."

Who would even do such a thing?

"It also looks like they took your personal effects," Violet said.

Tessa tightened her grip on the phone. "What?"

"I'm guessing when you left the house you had toiletries on your dresser or bathroom counter?" she asked. "Toothbrush, toothpaste, shampoo, hairbrush, hairspray, medications, makeup, stuff like that?"

"Yeah," Tessa said. "I probably left my dresser in a mess."

"Well, it's gone now," Violet said. "Along with what I'm guessing is half the clothes in your dresser. Judging by the indentations on the carpet in your closet, you also had a couple of large suitcases there, which they took too. The coatrack by your back door is also empty."

Tessa's head swam.

"What does that mean?" Anthony said. "What would they need with all that?"

"In my experience as an investigator with Missing Persons, a scene like this means that the person who lives here is on the run," Violet said bluntly. "I don't think they took it because they needed it but because they wanted to stage a scene. Right now this house looks as if Tessa packed up her life and ran. Do they have your wallet and cell phone too?"

"Yes," Tessa said.

Violet blew out a long breath.

"Tessa," she added, "to be blunt, I think that on the day Cassidy died, somebody planted evidence on her body to make it look like you had motive to kill her. Sure, they also went to the trouble of taking her cell phone and debit card on a journey so people would assume she was still alive. But framing you was in the killer's mind from the very beginning. Then today, when her body was found, somebody went to an awful lot of trouble to lure you to an island so that they could kidnap you. And now it's not enough that the police say you're on the run, somebody went into your house and staged your belongings to convince law enforcement that you planned to disappear. The fact they have your phone, wallet and belongings means that if they kill you, they can repeat the same trail of bread crumbs trick they tried to pull with Cassidy to make it look like you're alive and traipsing all over the globe."

"So, what do we do?" Anthony asked.

"I don't know," Violet admitted. "But, Tessa, I think whatever's going on begins and ends with you. I think Cassidy's killer is hoping you keep running and that they'll be the one to find you."

Anthony felt his footsteps drag beneath him as he climbed the stairs back up to Bert's cottage, as if they'd grown steeper since he'd walked down them. The contents of his phone calls with his sister and boss sat heavy in his mind. For a moment, he'd been so overwhelmed by the unexpected and foolhardy swell of emotion that had caused him to sweep Tessa up into his arms, he'd managed to push the reality of his situation aside. But now, with each step he felt it weighing heavier on him.

When he'd woken up this morning, it had been with the full certainty of who he was and what he was called to do with his life. Then, in a few hours, it had all been stripped away. He'd never really known what it was like to feel like he wasn't in charge of his own life, career and destiny. Now, his whole life was at the mercy of the very law enforcement agency he'd dedicated himself to. And the fact he didn't regret what he'd done didn't do anything to change how sad he was it had come to this, or how worried he was for his future.

Anthony and Tessa found Bert in the kitchen, where they told him about the conversations with Zablocie and Violet and filled their bowls with steaming chili and bread rolls. Then they walked into the living room, set up camp around an old steamer trunk that Bert cleared off to serve as a table, and ate while they worked the case. Although the food smelled amazing and Anthony could feel hunger rumbling in his stomach, every mouthful tasted like sawdust in his mouth.

For hours they passed printed pages from Tessa's files around between them, and filled a whiteboard with facts they knew and questions they had. With every investigative alley, Anthony could feel the loss of the weight and power of his badge, like the ache from a phantom limb. There were so many elements about the initial investigation into Cassidy's disappearance that he wanted to question colleagues about, and elements of the case he wanted a deeper perspective on. Time and again, as he met Tessa's eyes, somehow he could tell she was thinking similar things too. Slowly the sky grew from blue, to orange and red, then to a deep inky black outside the windows as the sun set beneath the trees. Finally, Tessa started yawning and suggested they all try to sleep for a bit and that maybe things would look different in the morning.

Bert told them the couch in the office folded out into a single bed. He suggested Anthony could sleep there, Tessa could have his room and he'd take the couch. But Tessa and Anthony objected immediately and said they weren't about to kick Bert out of his own room. After some debate and negotiation, it was decided that Bert would keep the comfort of his own bed, Anthony would stay in the living room and Tessa would take the office pullout, nestled between the computer, shelves and printer.

When Bert went to bed, leaving Anthony and Tessa alone in the living room, Anthony expected they'd sit up for a while and talk. But instead, Tessa hugged him goodnight moments after Bert's door had closed. Her lips brushed a kiss across Anthony's cheek.

"You're a good person, Anthony," she said, "and a terrific cop. I'm sorry I didn't really see the man you are on the inside sooner."

Then before he could say anything in response, she slipped from the room, went into the office and closed the door.

Silence fell, punctuated only by the ticking of the clock on the wall, insects chirping in the darkness and wind brushing the trees. Fatigue made his muscles ache. But sleep never came for Anthony. Instead, his mind continued to spin like a screeching engine pushed past its limits. He reread the case notes, double-checked all the doors, pulled a Bible from a shelf and tried to read it, laid down and closed his eyes, and then got back up and started the rotation all over again.

Lord, my gut tells me there's an answer here—to Cassidy's murder and to the entire mess we're in—that's so obvious we would've seen it long ago if only police had been look-ing in the right direction, listening to Tessa and taking her seriously.

The clock had already struck midnight when a dark shadow crossed the window. Anthony sat up sharply. There was someone outside the cabin. He scanned the room for a weapon and decided on a long and heavy flashlight. He slid his feet into his boots and laced them. Then he opened the door and stepped out into the night. The door lock clicked behind him. The day's storm had passed, leaving behind a clear and cloudless night. Darkness filled his eyes, and it took a few seconds for him to adjust to the moonlight. For a long moment he couldn't hear anyone and began to wonder if he'd been wrong.

Then he heard something rustling in the

trees ahead and to his right. Silently, he started through the trees toward the sound. The intruder was moving carefully and slowly and headed away from the house. Anthony held back and bided his time, waiting for the right moment to strike. A light flickered on ahead. Anthony stopped and pressed back against a tree. He heard the low murmur of a voice in the darkness. The figure seemed to be on a phone call. Anthony couldn't let him call for backup.

He leaped out from behind the trees, ran toward the figure and jumped, tackling the intruder to the ground. He heard a voice cry out, "Anthony! It's me!"

He got up. "Tessa?"

Her form was swamped in one of Bert's oversized hooded sweaters. Her hair fell loose around her shoulders. Her eyes were large in the moonlight. As she turned her face toward him, he realized she'd never looked more beautiful or felt so far away.

She stumbled to her feet. She had Bert's phone clutched in her hand, and it was only then Anthony realized that she'd never handed it back to him after talking with Violet. She slid the phone into her pocket.

"You can't stop me," she said. "It's already done."

Disappointment, frustration, anger and heartbreak crashed inside his heart in competing waves.

"What are you doing?" he asked. "How could you just take off and run after everything we've gone through?"

His voice rose. So did hers.

"I wasn't running," she said. "I called the police and turned myself in."

"You did what?"

No, she couldn't have. She'd spent all this time fighting to stay out of police custody and now she was just going to surrender?

"I walked away from the house in case they were able to locate the signal with GPS," she said. "I wanted to protect Bert by not placing the call inside his house, to give him plausible deniability if they accused him of harboring me. I thought I'd have enough time to place the call, come back to say goodbye to you and then walk far enough from Bert's house that they wouldn't target him. But they must've had someone closer than I realized because they said someone would pick me up in less than an hour."

He could hear the words she was saying, but somehow he didn't understand them or why everything inside him wanted to stop her.

"No," he said. He took both of her hands in his. "You can't clear your name or solve Cassidy's disappearance if you're sitting in a jail cell."

"Maybe not," Tessa said. She squeezed his hands tightly. "But you can. You said it yourself. The chief superintendent won't listen to you while I'm on the run. But if I turn myself in and clear your name, you'll be able to get back to work and solve this case."

His head shook as his mind scrambled for what to say.

"Tessa…" he started, but the word froze on his lips.

"I can't do it alone," she said. "I need help. I need you. And that means setting you free of the cloud of suspicion you're under. Please, Anthony. I've made so many mistakes and selfish decisions. Let me do the right thing. Let me rescue you, so that you can step up to help Cassidy and me."

He wanted to disagree with her. He wanted to argue. But she was right and he knew it. Zablocie didn't want to suspend Anthony or press charges against him. If Tessa turned herself in, Zablocie would be all too happy to reinstate him.

But…

"If you do this, I won't be able to contact

you," Anthony said. Sorrow filled his chest as the realization hit him. "There has to be a clean break. No visits. No letters. No calls or conversations. Even if Zablocie takes me off direct involvement in Cassidy's case. I can't be seen to be compromising the investigation."

"I know," Tessa said. She pulled her hands from his hands and slid them around his neck. "When I'm arrested, this is it for us. You need to protect yourself. You need to tell your boss the truth—that you tried to talk me into going in for questioning and eventually I realized you were right."

"But I don't want to lose you again." His voice grew husky in his throat.

"I don't want to lose you either," she said. "But I know it's the right thing to do."

"How can you be so sure?"

She laughed, sadly. "Because if the shoe was on the other foot, I know it's what you would do."

Tessa hugged him tightly. He hugged her back, but somehow they both stopped their lips from touching. Then they sat side by side on a fallen log and waited for her arrest.

"One of the people in my citizen detective group, Rowan, is a criminal defense lawyer," she said. "He lives in Calgary. Get Bert to call him. I'm sure he'll fly out."

He nodded. "I will."

He debated recommending lawyers but realized he was better off if she found her own.

"While I was trying to sleep, I was thinking about some of the clues you could chase up," she went on, and he had the impression she was trying to think of things to say to fill the time. "Remember how several witnesses reported seeing a guy and a girl trying to hitchhike north about an hour after Cassidy's friends left the bar? Police discounted it because they were heading the opposite direction from where her wallet and cell phone were located. But the cottage was in that direction. What if three of the young people had abandoned the other two, and they were forced to hitchhike? Or Cassidy was with someone and trying to get back to the cottage?"

"Good question," he said.

"Also, the Italian juniors roller-ski team posted a lot of pictures and videos on their way home from Whistler," she went on. "Bert pointed out it was a really good camera. I never looked into when or where they got it, but they didn't post much on the way there. Maybe one of them bought the camera in Whistler. There could be a clue there."

He nodded.

"I have a complete database of every known phone number, social media account and contact details for every single person involved in the case," she said. "Even Cassidy's five colleagues, the waitress at the bar, the owner of the grocery store across the street and the coach of the Italian roller-ski team. Maybe if you call them, as a cop, they'll talk to you and tell you things they weren't willing to tell me."

Anthony took her hand and squeezed it.

"Tessa," he said. "It's going to be okay. Trust me. I'm going to do everything in my power to make sure your name is cleared and Cassidy's murder is solved."

Even if he wouldn't be able to contact Tessa and tell her about it.

They lapsed back into silence. He could feel his heart weighed down by all the words he wished he could say and promises he wanted to make but didn't know if he could keep.

Then he saw headlights coming slowly down the road. She stood up and handed him back Bert's phone and sweater. His heart lurched.

"Please," he said. "Don't go."

Tears glistened in the corner of her eyes. "I have to."

"I know."

"This is bigger than you and me." She slid

her arms around him one final time. "And bigger than how I feel about you. Goodbye, Anthony."

A lump formed in his throat. He opened his mouth, but no words came out. Instead, he stepped back into the woods as Tessa ran through the trees toward the road. For one moment he saw her stand there, frozen with her hands above her head and her body illuminated in the headlights. Then both car doors opened, and he could see the red, yellow, white and blue RCMP stripes on the side.

"I am Tessa Watson," she called. "I'm surrendering!"

Anthony's heart pounded in his chest. Two uniformed RCMP officers got out, one male and one female. The female officer raised her weapon and yelled at Tessa to get down. She did so. Then the male officer approached, cuffed her, walked her to the car and put her in the back. The doors shut, and the car disappeared into the darkness.

Tessa was gone.

TWELVE

Tessa had never been arrested before, only threatened with it on occasion by cops who didn't want her to potentially impede their work and civilians who didn't want her nosing around in their business. But now that the moment had actually come, it was more awkward and surreal than she expected, as if she'd stopped being an individual the moment one of the officers flipped their police-issue notebook open and started reading her rights.

They explained that Tessa would be taken to a small local police station, where she'd be held without charges until an RCMP officer arrived from Vancouver to escort her there for processing. After which point, she'd be able to know the charges she was facing and also have her lawyer go before a judge to sort out if she was getting bail. Tessa fought the urge to explain that she knew they could hold her up to twenty-four hours before charging her. Instead, she said she understood and leaned back against the seat, trying to get comfortable with the handcuffs.

The police didn't speak to her or each other as they drove, leaving Tessa alone in the back with a bulletproof divider in front of her and the doors locked on either side. Tessa wondered if they'd both been dragged out of bed in the middle of the night to come get her. Monotony began to creep in. It was so dark outside, all she could see was her own face reflected back in the glass, leaving her with nothing to distract her from her own troubled thoughts and the fear in the pit of her stomach.

Finally, they reached the police station. It was a tiny, single-story building sitting like a cupboard box on a highway in the middle of nowhere. They took her inside, fingerprinted her, took her photo, patted her down, took away anything she could use to hurt herself, and then they showed her into the small cell that would be her home for the night. It was about a quarter of the size of a bedroom, with plain tile floors, a tiny window and a cot attached to the wall that didn't so much as have a blanket on it. They wished her good night and told her that there would be an officer on duty just around the corner in case of emergency. Then they left her alone.

And that was when the full force of what she'd just done finally hit her.

She'd felt trapped before in her life, but nothing like this, and the knowledge that she was now stuck in one small room with no way to leave gripped her lungs, painfully stealing her breath. Her heart raced and beat into her throat until she thought she would choke.

When she'd been grounded as a teenager she'd always known there was a window she could climb out of. Every night now, back in her apartment, she'd fall asleep at night to the sound of rushing water or music playing. When she'd been stuck in a waiting room, there'd always been a book, her telephone or television to distract her. But now she had none of that. Not even a pencil and piece of paper to scribble on. For the first time in her life she was well and truly alone with her thoughts and no way to distract herself from them.

The negative and critical thoughts hit her first, battering her with every mistake she'd ever made and nasty thing she'd ever been told, or even thought, about herself. But now, with no way to push the thoughts away, she had no choice but to turn them over to God.

Lord, You said we shouldn't be quick to anger and I have been so many times. I'm sorry for how I lashed out at Cassidy when she chose Kevin over me. I'm sorry I judged her instead of listening and telling her I'd be there for her no matter what. I hate how I then pushed Anthony away. I never wanted him to go, and then I blamed him for leaving instead of fighting to stay. I don't like how judgmental and stubborn I've been. I want to repair my relationship with my parents, but I don't know how. I want to stop pushing people away.

Words from the Bible's 1 Corinthians 13 filled her mind and she claimed them as her own.

I want to be patient and kind. I want to stop being envious and thinking about myself. I want to stop being quick to anger and stop being so easily provoked.

She wanted to be more like Anthony. Not that she wanted to stop being herself, but she wanted his good qualities to rub off on her too. She wanted him in her life. She prayed for Anthony too, and that God would guide his investigation and that he'd be reinstated quickly.

And, oh, how she missed him!

Yet, with each prayer she felt more certain that she'd done the right thing by turning herself in. She had faith that one day, months or even years from now, she would be cleared and Cassidy's killer would be found and face justice.

Finally, as the hours stretched on and sleep still refused to come, she prayed for her own future and that God would take the entire mess she was in and turn it into something beautiful.

She didn't even realize she'd actually managed to fall asleep until she heard an odd rumbling roar fill the air. She opened her eyes and sat up. It was still dark outside, with a faint gray of approaching dawn around the edges of the horizon.

A male officer who she hadn't seen before appeared at the door to her cell.

"What time is it?" she asked.

"Five thirty," the officer said. "Your lawyer is here to see you."

"My lawyer?" Bert had managed to get Rowan in that quickly?

"Yup, he flew in by helicopter," he said. "He's worked out a deal with the RCMP to escort you directly to Vancouver, where you will be charged and processed."

"Really?" That was way too fast to be believable.

"He'll meet with you in the briefing room,"

the officer went on. "You will see cameras in the room, but they'll be turned off to comply with lawyer-client confidentiality requirements."

She thanked the officer and followed him out of the cell, down a long hallway and into a plain room with gray walls, a rectangular table, two plastic chairs and a couple of water bottles. A tall man stood at the far end in a sharp gray suit, talking on a phone, with his back to her. The officer left, and the door locked behind her.

The man turned and she blinked. At first she didn't even recognize the handsome figure with a bright white smile.

"Nice to see you, Tessa." He waved her toward a chair, and she saw the smudgy black tattoo on the inside of his wrist. "Just keep calm, stay civilized, do what I say and everything will be okay."

It was the man in the white hat and mask, who'd rented her the canoe, shot Anthony and tried his best to kidnap her over and over again. What was he thinking, showing up and posing as her lawyer? He had to know police were just outside the door. She squinted slightly.

"Cole Rook, right?" she asked. "I thought you just represented drunk drivers and men who picked on people who are weaker than them." She kept her eyes locked on his face, but with her peripheral vision she scanned the room for anything she could use as a weapon. "I'm not going anywhere with you," she said, "and I'm not going to let you lay a hand on me."

His wide and toothy smile tightened slightly at the edges.

"I'm not going to hurt you," he said. "I'm not that kind of guy."

He sounded almost offended that she'd suggested it, which was laughable. She took a deep breath. As long as she was within the police station she was safe. He had to know she could tell police anything he told her.

"Tell that to Cassidy Chase," she said.

"I never laid a hand on Cassidy."

He stepped toward her. She moved slowly around the table to make sure it stayed between them.

"I told you at the beginning of all this that I wouldn't hurt you if you cooperated," he said.

She snorted. "Well, I'm not about to cooperate now."

"You sure about that?" He placed a small computer tablet down on the table with a self-satisfied flourish. "We have your boyfriend."

"I don't believe you—"

But her words froze as she looked at the screen and saw a video of Anthony's truck. He was pulling into what looked like a loading dock. Where was he? What was he doing there? He stepped out of the truck, still in the exact same clothes he'd been wearing when she saw him last, and started toward a door. Two masked figures leaped out of the darkness and attacked him. Anthony was knocked to the ground. One of them held a rag to his face, and the other knelt on his back until Anthony went limp. Her heart caught in her throat. The video time stamp said it had happened less than twenty minutes ago.

It didn't make sense. Why was he skulking around what looked like an underground parking lot in the exact same clothes he'd worn the night before? Why wasn't he in uniform? Why did he look disheveled, like he'd slept in his truck? It didn't make any sense.

"I don't believe it," she said. "That can't be real."

Cole smirked, pushed a button on his tablet and initiated a video call. Seconds later Lewis answered it.

"Yo, what's up?" Lewis's face filled the

screen. He looked like he was in some kind of warehouse.

"I've got Tessa with me," Cole said. "I want you to show her our friend."

Lewis chuckled and moved the camera around so she could see. There Anthony lay on the hard cement floor, looking the same as he had in the video. His eyes were closed, but when Lewis kicked him hard in the shins he moaned faintly.

She felt her face pale.

"I want you to set a ten minute timer," Cole told Lewis. "If I don't call you back within the next ten minutes and show you I'm on my way in the helicopter with Tessa, I want you to shoot him. Got it?"

"Got it."

"See you in ten." Cole ended the call and turned back to Tessa. "I didn't want to have to do this. I'm a nice guy, and I didn't want to have to resort to this, but you really gave me no choice. I need you to come with me, so we can sit down and have a nice little chat about what happened to Cassidy Chase all those years ago and what's going to happen about it now. So, in a minute I'm going to open that door, the police are going to release you into my custody, and we're going to walk back to my helicopter together. If you try to escape, or get me arrested, or even signal to the police in any way, Anthony will die."

The smell of chloroform was sickly sweet in Anthony's lungs and made his tongue feel heavy. He'd never had anyone try to drug him before or taken anything stronger than an aspirin for pain. But even though he'd been able to tell the rag his masked attacker had stuffed in his face had probably contained a lighter dose than was needed for someone Anthony's size, he wasn't in a hurry to relive the experience. So he lay, slumped on the floor where they'd left him, biding his time and praying.

Anthony had placed a whole lot of phone calls between running back to the house to wake up Bert, and pulling into the nondescript underground entrance of a downtown Vancouver high-rise, where he'd promptly been leaped upon by two men in ski masks. It had been slightly after one thirty in the morning when he'd placed a call to the number Tessa's files identified as Kevin Scotch-Simmond's cell phone. He'd left a message identifying himself as Sergeant Anthony Jones of the RCMP, and said he had uncovered information relating to the night Cassidy Chase disappeared. The response had been a text at four forty-two in the morning instructing him to be at a Vancouver skyscraper's loading dock in fifteen minutes. Thankfully, he'd already been back in Vancouver and had made the rendezvous with moments to spare.

Only to then spend what he guessed was half an hour laid out on the cold concrete floor, waiting.

A voice he recognized as Lewis's seemed to be responding to directions from someone on the phone. Then he was dragged to his feet by Drew, who held him up, and Lewis searched him thoroughly for both weapons and wires, and confiscated his cell phone. Anthony wobbled as if he had sea legs.

But where was the third member of the trio, Cole Rook?

"All clear," Lewis said.

They led him through a plain and unimpressive hallway, and into an elevator. The building was sixty-four stories tall, judging by the numbers on the buttons. Drew hit the button labeled Upper Penthouse. The elevator started to rise. It opened up to a small landing aggressively decorated in orange and white, with a single door that Anthony guessed was wood, which someone had paid an awful lot of money to make look like metal.

It clicked open when Lewis tapped on it, and they ushered Anthony inside.

He'd expected to walk into something resembling a living room. And while the large square room that he found himself in definitely had multiple couches, continuing the theme of being inside an orange, there was also a large black desk straight ahead. It was in front of a wall that consisted entirely of floor-to-ceiling windows that looked out on the beautiful Vancouver skyline, Vancouver Island and, beyond that, the Pacific Ocean.

The door locked automatically behind him. They led him to a white leather chair in front of the desk. He sat. It was incredibly uncomfortable, with a straight back, slippery surface and no armrests, and Anthony found he had to dig his heels into the floor to keep up the appearance that he was still kind of dazed without actually sliding off completely. Drew and Lewis hesitated, and he noticed they kept glancing at a door to the right of the desk, as if they expected someone to walk through it.

Then they went to stand by the wall. Still no Cole.

The deep rumble of an approaching helicopter shook the air. The sound grew closer until the glass windows rippled, and then he heard it land. It seemed someone was making an entrance. A door to the left of the desk opened, and Kevin Scotch-Simmonds walked in, wearing a pair of green sweatpants and a Vegas Golden Knights T-shirt. Anthony fought the urge to point out that he didn't match the room's color scheme.

Kevin was shorter than Anthony had remembered. Back then, the kind of life Kevin had been living hadn't quite caught up to him or stolen his youthful glow. But now it was clear that Kevin was only a few years short of forty. He had the muscles of a man who took illegal supplements and the blond hair of someone who paid a lot of money to get rid of the gray. His teeth were unnaturally white, and his skin was unnaturally tan. Anthony could see why his more photogenic brother and parents were the ones who appeared on Scotch-Simmonds cookie boxes and ice cream.

"Sergeant Jones, so nice to meet you!" Kevin said.

Huh. As Anthony analyzed the man's face for signs of dishonesty, he realized to his surprise that Kevin was actually telling the truth. Kevin honestly did think he'd never met Anthony before. Then again, maybe he'd edited out of his memory the skinny young man who'd once laid him out on the ground when taking Tessa and Cassidy home. What's more, Kevin actually seemed pleased, as if he thought he'd already won before stepping into the ring. He sat down behind the desk.

"Are you okay?" Kevin asked. "I heard two masked thugs jumped you in the garage! Crime is getting so bad in this city. I'm so thankful that my friends were there to rescue you and help you upstairs."

And now here came the lies. Anthony had occasionally taught a workshop for other interrogators on how to tell if someone was being deceitful. And from the way Kevin's hands fidgeted, his eyes darted around the room and his tone rose and fell, the man was the perfect example of someone lying through their teeth.

Anthony rolled his aching jaw for a beat and wondered just how gullible Kevin Scotch-Simmonds thought he was.

"Funny," Anthony said. "I thought it was your friends that jumped me."

Kevin tried not to smirk and failed.

"You can't possibly know that," he said. "I saw on security footage that they were masked."

"Well, one of them did take my phone," Anthony pointed out.

"Couldn't risk you trying to get sneaky and record me," Kevin said. He leaned back. "So, you have some new evidence about how Cassidy Chase died?"

"No, actually I don't," Anthony admitted.

Kevin blinked rapidly, as if someone had just tossed a glass of ice water in his face. He leaned forward, with both elbows on the table. "So, you're not here to try and toss around some new evidence about her death?"

"No, I'm not," Anthony confirmed. "The honest truth is, I still have no idea how Cassidy Chase died."

Kevin let out a long breath.

"What I'm here to talk about is money," Anthony said and leaned forward.

"Money?" Kevin repeated.

His eyes darted to a door at Anthony's right. It was the same one Lewis and Drew had been glancing at earlier. Now Anthony could see it was open a crack.

Was somebody there?

"Did you know it's currently late afternoon in Italy?" Anthony said. "I had an interesting chat with somebody there a couple of hours ago. Apparently, the evening Cassidy Chase disappeared a member of the Italian junior roller-ski team was approached by a stranger in an incredibly nice car, who asked him for a favor."

Kevin leaned forward again. Something dangerous glinted in his eyes.

"The stranger told the kid that he'd driven up to Whistler to surprise his girlfriend, and asked him to go into a bar and tell her that he was outside waiting for her. In exchange, the stranger offered the boy a beautiful new digital camera as a thank-you."

"What an interesting story," Kevin said. "Did the boy ever tell this tale to police?"

"No," Anthony said. "Because it wasn't until months later that he realized the woman he'd talked to, Cassidy Chase, had disappeared. He was worried what his parents would think when they found out about the camera, especially because his family's struggling orchard had recently struck a big deal with a Canadian grocery store company, and they didn't want the bad publicity of their son being involved in a crime. So, he convinced himself she was probably fine."

Kevin looked like he wanted to say something, but Anthony didn't give him the opportunity.

"Speaking of which, Cassidy's friend Katie Masters had a similar experience with regret that night," Anthony said. "It's late morning now out on the East Coast. See, she'd gone off alone with Tom Groff after they'd left the bar, and she'd done some foolish things she wasn't particularly proud of, especially as she had a serious boyfriend, who she's married to now, and didn't believe in doing drugs. Katie and Tom were the pair that witnesses saw hitchhiking back to the cottage. When she realized the police and the media were going to scrutinize every moment of her night, her friend Cole said he'd have her back, her secret was safe with them, and they'd all agree to tell anyone who asked that they'd all left together. After all, Cassidy was probably fine, and why drag Katie's life through the mud? She cried as she told me the story. I think she was relieved to finally tell it. A wonderful friend reminded me recently how shame can sabotage our ability to truly live."

Anthony heard either Lewis or Drew shift their weight from one foot to the other. But Anthony kept his eyes locked on Kevin.

Kevin smiled like a man with a dagger up his sleeve. "And did anyone give Katie or her family money?"

"No," Anthony said. "But Tom got a random lump sum of five thousand dollars a few months later, and you have been making regular payments to Cole, Drew and Lewis ever since."

Kevin's smile faded in an instant.

"My theory is you got that poor Italian kid to lure Cassidy from the bar and take her back to the cottage, where you killed her," Anthony said. "When Cole, Drew and Lewis came back, they found you there, and you paid them to lie and say you were never there."

Thunder filled Kevin's face. He leaped to his feet and scrambled around for something on his desk. He snatched up the item, and Anthony leapt to his feet too, thinking it was a gun. Instead, it was a television remote. Kevin aimed it at a large flat-screen on the side of the room and fired. The screen sprang to life. It was frozen on a news channel, like someone had been watching live television a few minutes before Anthony had walked into the room and had paused it for dramatic effect. There stood Chief Superintendent Zablocie on the steps of the RCMP headquarters before dawn, with a dozen reporters' microphones stuck in his face. The red news ticker underneath his image announced a nationwide manhunt was underway for disgraced officer Sergeant Anthony Jones, who was suspected of destroying evidence and aiding and abetting a killer.

Anthony sat back down again. The door to his right creaked open another inch. Whoever was on the other side was listening.

Kevin stabbed the remote with his thumb again, and the picture began to play.

"...Sergeant Anthony Jones is considered armed and extremely dangerous. Anyone who thinks they've seen Sergeant Jones should not approach him but instead call 911—"

Kevin paused the television again.

"You think I'm stupid?" Kevin practically seethed. He was still standing over Anthony. "You think I don't watch TV and follow the internet? Your face popped up all over social media less than an hour after you called and left me a message saying you were a cop who'd uncovered information about the night Cassidy Chase disappeared. You lied to me. You're not a cop anymore. You're a criminal. A fugitive. You don't have any evidence I hurt Cassidy, or for anything else you claim you've found. You know police won't arrest me on some twelve-year-old witness statement alone. So you came here, pretending you're still a cop, in the hopes of tricking me into confessing to save yourself."

"You're right," Anthony said. "I was suspended."

Kevin laughed triumphantly.

"But you're forgetting what I told you just a couple of minutes ago," Anthony went on. "I'm not here about evidence of a murder. I'm here about money."

He let that last word fall into the space between them.

Kevin sat.

"You pay people to cover up for you," Anthony said. "Those two men sitting behind me?" He turned and gestured at Lewis and Drew. "They're not your friends, and they're not your employees. They're your captors. Them and Cole Rook. You're not bribing them, if that's what you're telling yourself. They're blackmailing you and that makes you weak." Anthony leaned back. "And I want in. I want you to make me an offer. I want you to offer to pay me for the rest of my life, to keep what I know about you to myself."

Kevin snorted. But despite the bravado, Anthony could read the fear in his eyes.

"If that were true," Kevin said, "what's to stop me from just killing you right here and now?"

"You need me," Anthony said. "I can help

you. I'm not your enemy here. Tessa is. You didn't get every copy of her database. I still have a copy. She dedicated her life to proving you killed her best friend, and now I have everything she found. And if I can turn up all this new information in just a few hours, imagine what I can discover in days."

Anthony stood, walked over to Kevin's desk, braced his hands on the shining wood and looked down at him.

"A former cop in your pocket is a lot more valuable to you than a dead one," Anthony said. "I still know how to work the system. I have access and I know how to get you things you never even dreamed of. Plus think of all the ways I'll be able to help you when my suspension is over and I'm reinstated."

Kevin opened his mouth, but no words came out. His hands shook with what Anthony sensed was a mixture of fear and rage.

The door to the right of the room finally swung open, Tessa walked through, and Anthony's heart froze. Her hands were bound at the wrists with zip ties, and there was a bandana tied around her mouth. Cole had one strong hand on her shoulders and a knife to the side of her throat. As her hazel eyes locked on Anthony's face, he knew they'd made sure she'd heard every word. Cole pressed into her shoulder until she whimpered and dropped to her knees.

Kevin turned to Anthony.

"You're not the only one with leverage," Kevin said. "If you really want to join my team, you can start by killing Tessa for me."

THIRTEEN

As Tessa raised her head, looked straight across the room past her kidnappers and into Anthony's deep blue eyes, she knew that, whatever happened next, she trusted him with her entire heart. Even as Cole had held her on the other side of the door, ensuring she heard every word of Anthony and Kevin's conversation, she'd never doubted Anthony for a minute. The man she'd given her heart to so many years ago would protect her, fight for her and make sure she was safe. She believed in him. And as silent emotion swelled in the depths of Anthony's gaze, she could see he knew it too.

"Are you surprised?" Kevin asked Anthony. He was gloating now, like a child who had pulled off a magic trick.

"I am," Anthony said. "A bit. I mean it's been pretty clear from the get-go you were using Tessa to throw suspicion off yourself.

I didn't really think anything of it when she first told me she'd been stalked and followed for years. But that was you, wasn't it? Keeping tabs on her. Keeping her afraid. You planted her letter on Cassidy's body. Then when the body was found, you lured her to the island so you could kidnap her and make it look like she'd gone on the run, so everybody would stay focused on her. You even got someone to stage her house to make it look like she'd fled. But what I don't understand is why Tessa? Why her? You could've framed any number of people who were actually in Whistler that weekend far more easily. Some random waiter or drifter. If it had been me, I'd have targeted one of the guys who was up at the cottage that weekend and tried to turn him against the others."

"She made Cassidy leave me," Kevin said. "I drove all the way up to surprise her, and instead Cassidy told me that she couldn't be with me anymore because Tessa had poisoned her mind against me."

Sudden tears sprung to Tessa's eyes. Cassidy hadn't died hating her.

"So, you killed her," Anthony said.

"She got hysterical," Kevin said. "I tried to make her see reason, and there was an accident."

Right. Tessa was oddly thankful she'd been spared the details of how her friend had died.

"If we're going to do this," Anthony said, "I need to know how you wiped out her databases. You don't have the skills for that, and neither do Lewis, Drew or Cole."

"I hired some guy from the dark web who's good at making things disappear," Kevin said with a shrug.

Anthony's arms crossed.

"I want twenty-five thousand up front," he said. "Then we'll renegotiate depending if you need me to do more things for you. More when I get reinstated with the RCMP. Unless you already have someone within law enforcement working for you. In which case, I need to know now."

"I've got nobody in law enforcement," Kevin said. He ran his hand over his jaw, as if it hadn't even occurred to him before what a good idea that would be. "Again, stop stalling."

Kevin opened another drawer, pulled out what looked like a handgun and offered it to Anthony. He took it without hesitation. Cole pulled the knife away from Tessa's neck and stepped back to join Lewis and Drew, taking himself far out of the line of fire.

"Well, I think we're done here," Anthony said. "I've got everything I came for."

Then he turned to Tessa. She looked up at Anthony.

"I'm sorry, Tessa," he said.

He aimed the weapon between her eyes and pulled the trigger.

A metallic click sounded from the gun that reminded her of a finger snap.

"Dude, I'm a cop." Anthony shot Kevin a withering glance. "This isn't a real gun. Did you really think I wouldn't be able to tell the difference between an actual firearm and a non-firing replica?"

"You think I'm dumb enough to trust you?" Kevin asked. His smile was slimy and smug. The fact he seemed to be enjoying this made Tessa's skin crawl. "I don't need you to kill her. I just need video evidence of you aiming a gun at her head so that if her body's ever found you'll be framed for it! This whole place is wired with cameras." Kevin snatched another gun from inside his desk. "Besides, I've been really looking forward to killing her myself."

But before he could even raise it to aim, a gunshot sounded from the far side of the room. The bullet flew through the window beside Kevin's head, shattering the glass. Tessa looked to see who had fired it. Her jaw dropped.

It was Drew.

"Everybody down!" Drew shouted. "This is a police sting operation! I've been recording everything!"

Chaos erupted. She heard the sound of police pounding at the main door, threatening to break it down. Cole threw himself at Drew. Lewis fired toward Anthony and struck the television screen. It exploded.

But Anthony dove for Tessa, enveloped her into his arms and pulled her back behind the door. He slammed it and locked it behind them. He pulled the gag from her lips, and she gasped for breath.

"Police have staked out around the building," he said. "They've got the whole place surrounded. We've just got to hold tight until police secure the scene and give the all clear. Thankfully Drew has a bulletproof vest on, and we've got paramedics on standby."

He glanced around. The room was a swanky lounge area, with a wet bar to their left and sliding glass doors on their left that led out to a rooftop pool.

"Sorry, that was all a little more theatrical

than I was expecting," he added. He grabbed a pair of scissors off a counter and cut her wrists free.

"They were supposed to barge in after I tricked him into confessing and he agreed to my blackmail demand. I hadn't expected Kevin to have a hostage."

"Cole showed up at the station posing as my lawyer and threatened to kill you if I didn't go with him," she said.

"And so you came," he said.

"Of course."

"I found Drew hiding out at his grandmother's house," he said, "thanks to a tip in your files, and talked him into being a hero."

"You did say you'd turn him," she said.

"He really did want to be a good guy," Anthony said. "Then all that was left to pull off the sting was wake up Zablocie in the middle of the night and convince him to agree to the operation and personally destroy me on television."

A bullet ripped through the door they'd just escaped through, sending splinters flying. Anthony grabbed her hand, and they ran through the lounge, out the double glass doors and on to rooftop patio.

A second bullet sounded behind them. Fresh

morning air filled their lungs. The patio area was surprisingly small, with a waist-high glass wall surrounding the perimeter and thin wire chairs. The helicopter pad lay to their left.

Tessa's chest tightened. They were so very high up off the ground. There was nowhere to hide, the police hadn't secured the scene yet and neither of them had a weapon.

"You're not going to get away with this, Tessa!" Kevin shouted. They turned to see Kevin striding out onto the rooftop. A hatred filled his eyes that bordered on manic. He raised his gun with both hands and aimed it toward them. "I'm not going to let you ruin my life!"

He pulled the trigger, and Anthony leaped at him. For a moment she watched as they struggled for the gun. Then Kevin threw himself toward the glass barrier, it broke and the two men tumbled over the edge of the building.

"Anthony!" she screamed.

She ran for the edge of the skyscraper by the hole in the fence where the men had crashed through.

"Tessa, help!" Anthony clung to a twisted piece of the broken railing an arm's length beneath her. She dropped to her stomach, reached down and grabbed his closest wrist with both hands. Kevin clung to his knees, pummeling the air with swear words and promising to tell her everything she wanted to know about exactly how he killed Cassidy if they pulled him up. Then she looked past him to a wide balcony about two stories below, where three muscular RCMP agents were reaching up and prepared to catch him.

"Kick him off!" she shouted. "It'll be all right. Someone will catch him! Trust me!"

Anthony kicked back hard and shook Kevin free. Kevin screamed in terror. But then she felt Anthony's strong hand grab ahold of her forearms and she steadied his weight as he climbed back up.

Anthony and Tessa collapsed side by side on the roof and gasped for breath. He looked down and so did she. Kevin was sprawled safely on the balcony below them, shouting that his ankle was sprained as officers hand-cuffed him. Then Anthony took Tessa's hand and led her away from the edge and toward a chair. He sat, pulled her onto his lap and wrapped his arms around her. Together they looked out at the morning sun streaming over the mountains.

"Are you okay?" Anthony asked.

"Please never stop asking me that," Tessa